The Thin Blue Line Series

THE DUSTY ROAD TO HOMICIDE

LeeAnne James

Black Rose Writing | Texas

The author grants the final approval for this literary material.

First printing

This is a work of fiction. Names, characters, businesses, places, events, and incidents are either the products of the author's imagination or used in a fictitious manner. Any resemblance to actual persons, living or dead, or actual events is purely coincidental.

ISBN: 978-1-68513-260-6
PUBLISHED BY BLACK ROSE WRITING
www.blackrosewriting.com

Printed in the United States of America
Suggested Retail Price (SRP) $20.95

The Dusty Road to Homicide is printed in Calluna

*As a planet-friendly publisher, Black Rose Writing does its best to eliminate unnecessary waste to reduce paper usage and energy costs, while never compromising the reading experience. As a result, the final word count vs. page count may not meet common expectations.

I'd like to dedicate *The Dusty Road to Homicide* to my mother. Towards the end, while she was in the nursing home, she did not recognize me but as she spoke to me - the unfamiliar visitor in her room - she would say that her "daughter is a published author." Her memory may not have been present, but the pride was.

Acknowledgements

I'd like to send my family a world of thanks for listening to my plot ideas and helping me to improve on them. I'm a firm believer that everything can always be tweaked, and you've helped me tweak my books to make them much better than they were when I first began.

Once again, I must thank Luke for being my technical advisor. You've made sure that everything is as it should be when it comes to police procedures.

THE DUSTY ROAD TO HOMICIDE

You were not born a winner, and you were not born a loser. You are what you make yourself to be.
–Lou Holtz, Football player and coach

Our prime purpose in this life is to help others and if you can't help them, at least don't hurt them.
–Dalai Lama

CHAPTER ONE

Four-year-old Dusty Sampson was hiding under the front porch, shaking so badly, his teeth were chattering. He pulled his knees up to his chest, wrapping his thin arms tightly around his bony legs. He couldn't tell if he'd peed his pants, or if the wetness was from the dampness of the soil he was sitting in.

He didn't like it when his parents argued. They were arguing a lot lately and as a result, Dusty found himself hiding under the porch more and more. He didn't like being under the porch, but listening to his parents yelling at each other was worse than being near the cobwebs that hung from the wooden beams over his head. He tried closing his eyes and putting his hands over his ears, but it didn't help. Dusty could still hear them shouting, and he knew the cobwebs were still there. He didn't like the musty smell of the old, wet wood under the porch, either. It was an awful smell and sometimes it made him sneeze.

Dusty heard the screen door as it banged against the wall above his head. He jumped at the sudden loud sound and pulled his knobby knees tighter to his chest, trying to make himself even smaller. He could see the heels of his father's dirty boots as he stomped down the decrepit, open steps and down the dirt path that led to the street. The door banged above his head again, but this time, it was his mother who came out. Dusty listened as she yelled at his father and his father yelled back. Then he heard the car start, and a loud, screeching noise as his father drove away. He heard the screen door slam again, so he knew his mother must have gone back inside. A single tear left a wet trail down his cheek. He laid his head on his knees and let the tears fall.

Dusty didn't understand all the words that his parents had been screaming at each other, but he knew they weren't nice words. Mom said that Daddy had a girlfriend and Mom didn't like her. She called the girlfriend a bitch and a whore. Dusty didn't know what that meant, but he figured they were bad words because it made daddy mad when Mommy said it. But then Daddy would say Mommy was full of shit. Dusty knew that was a bad word, too.

Dusty stayed under the porch a little while longer until the yelling and his tears had stopped for sure and he knew it was safe to come out. When they got into arguments in the past, Daddy usually took off for the rest of the day, and Mommy would go into their bedroom and close the door. Sometimes Dusty heard noises that sounded like Mommy was crying. That made him sad.

He tried hard to stay quiet and not bother her. Sometimes she stayed in there until it was past his bedtime. When that happened, she would forget to make something for Dusty's dinner, so Dusty would fix himself a bowl of cereal. He was getting good at that. He hardly ever spilled the milk anymore.

Dusty woke up the next morning to find that Daddy hadn't come home. His mother was at the kitchen table, smoking cigarettes and drinking coffee. She had a mountainous pile of wadded up tissues on the table in front of her.

"Where's Daddy?" Dusty asked quietly. He stood at the table, still in the mismatched pajama top and bottoms he'd pulled from the dresser drawer the night before.

"How the hell should I know? He's probably with his whore." Dusty's mom snubbed out her cigarette in the overflowing ashtray and lit another one. "Are you hungry, baby?"

"Yes, Mommy. I'm real hungry." His small hand instinctively went to his stomach.

"Just get yourself a bowl of cereal and a glass of milk and go watch TV. I need to think." She took a deep drag off her cigarette. Dusty watched as she blew out a thick line of smoke. He followed it with his eyes as it melded with the smoke that floated above their heads like a wavy, gray cloud.

Dusty reached for the box of cereal that was in the same place on the counter where he'd left it the night before. Last night's dirty bowl and spoon were also on the counter next to the cereal. Dusty used them again. He dumped some cereal into the bowl, got his favorite Pokemon mug from the sink, and poured milk into the mug and on his cereal.

Making two trips, he carefully carried his bowl of cereal and mug of milk to the living room, and set them on the coffee table. He turned on the TV, settling for reruns of Peppa Pig. He knew to keep the volume down low so the noise wouldn't bother Mommy.

·   ·   ·   ·   ·

Two weeks went by, and Dusty's father still hadn't come home. He'd never been gone this long before.

"Mommy," Dusty asked softly, "when is Daddy coming home?" His bottom lip began to quiver.

"He's not coming home, baby. He shacked up with his new girlfriend, the whore."

Dusty turned away before his mother could see the tears spilling from his eyes and running down his cheeks. He missed his daddy.

For a long time, when he and his mother went to the grocery store or Walmart, Dusty would look at the men in the store, trying to see if he could find his father. When he walked on the sidewalk and men passed by, Dusty would look to find recognition in their eyes.

He would ask about his father many times over the next few years but his mother always said the same thing, that his father had left them to fend for themselves, that he didn't care about Dusty or her, and that he was shacked up with his whore and would never be coming home.

Eventually Dusty stopped asking, but deep down, he never stopped hoping his father would return.

CHAPTER TWO

Dusty sat at the kitchen table, struggling to do his homework. The third-grade math homework wasn't difficult, but Earl, his mother's latest boyfriend, was watching a baseball game on the television and couldn't watch any type of sports without yelling loudly and swearing at the players. It didn't matter what sport or which teams were playing. He would throw a fit, no matter who or what was on TV.

Dusty had never been able to concentrate when he was surrounded by a lot of noise - especially yelling - or anything else that caused a distraction for him. He had that problem a lot. His teacher, Mrs. Hinkle, had a name for it... attention deficit something or other. She said he was smart enough to do the work, but he had a hard time paying attention. It was times like this that he understood what she meant.

Earl had been living with his mother and Dusty for about six months. Dusty didn't like Earl because all he ever did was sit around, drink beer, and watch television. He didn't even have a job. And yet, his mother was working as a waitress at the Silver Dollar

Diner for as many hours as she could get, just to pay the bills. Dusty hardly ever got to see her anymore. When she wasn't working, she was either sleeping, or she was too busy with Earl.

Dusty didn't like the way Earl was always grabbing at his mother, putting his hands on her butt or her boobs. Sometimes when his mother was tired, she would push him away, but other times she would laugh, especially after she'd had a couple of beers with Earl. Then they would go into the bedroom, lock the door, and Dusty would hear Earl grunting and his mother shrieking.

One time, he asked his mother what they were doing, but his mother told him to mind his own business. It didn't sound like she was getting hurt, so he let it go. But if he ever found out that Earl hurt his mom, Dusty knew he would punch Earl as hard as his eight-year-old fists could punch.

He closed his math book with a sigh. He would not get his homework done that night and there was no point in trying. The next day at school, Dusty knew he had a free period before his math class. Maybe he could try to get his homework done then.

He wanted to get good grades and make his mother proud. Maybe if he did, she would pay more attention to him, like she used to do when there weren't any boyfriends living with them.

Oh! Dusty just remembered that tomorrow was class picture day, so he ran into his bedroom to see if he had any clean shirts left. He found one under his bed, but it was an old Pokemon tee shirt with a picture of Pikachu on the front and Charizard on the back. He swiped at the dust bunnies that clung to the material. Dusty looked closely at the shirt. He still liked the shirt, but now it was too small for him. Besides, if he wore it to school, the other kids might pick on him and call him a baby. He threw it back under the bed.

Later that night, Dusty's mom got home after working a double-shift at the diner. He knew better than to bother her as soon as she got home, especially after she worked a sixteen-hour day. She was usually very tired and needed time to unwind, but he was eager to talk to her. He wanted to ask if she knew of any clean shirts he could wear for his class picture.

Sometimes, if his mother worked the evening shift, she would bring leftovers home from the diner. Dusty was happy that tonight was one of those times. He liked the food from the diner. He saw her carry in the big bag that said Silver Dollar Diner on the side and followed her into the kitchen, where she dropped the bag onto the table.

While his mother went into her bedroom to change out of her uniform, Dusty climbed onto a kitchen chair so he'd be tall enough to get the shiny aluminum takeout containers out of the brown paper bag. He carefully pried the cardboard covers off each one. She'd brought home fried chicken with green beans and cornbread in one container, a couple slices of meatloaf with more green beans, mashed potatoes and gravy in the second container, and a bacon cheeseburger with French fries in the third container.

Earl sauntered in from the living room, a lit cigarette dangling from the corner of his mouth. A long bit of ash fell from the end of the cigarette, bounced off his protruding stomach, and landed on the floor. Earl didn't even notice. He looked over the containers and took the one with the cheeseburger and fries without asking if anyone else might want it. With a loud belch, he grabbed another beer out of the refrigerator and brought his meal into the living room. He sat down in front of the television with the container of food balanced on his lap.

Dusty waited for his mother, who came out of the bedroom in pajamas and a bathrobe. He was standing on the chair with both hands on the table as he leaned over the two remaining takeout containers. "Which one do you want, Mom?"

"I don't care, baby. Take whichever one you want." She reached into the fridge and grabbed a bottle of beer. She twisted off the cap and tossed it towards the overflowing garbage bin. It bounced off the pile of garbage, landed with a clink on the floor, and rolled under the table. She left it there.

"Can I have the fried chicken?" asked Dusty, a big smile revealing the missing tooth on the bottom that had fallen out the week before.

"Sure. That's fine." His mother sat at the table across from Dusty and took a long pull from the beer.

Dusty climbed down from the chair and found two forks in the utensil drawer. He gave one to his mother and kept the other. He returned to his chair and pushed the container with the meatloaf towards her. She quietly nodded her thanks. Then he pulled the container with the chicken towards himself and sat at the table directly across from his mother, their usual seats.

They ate in silence, Dusty enjoying his fried chicken, his mother only picking at the meatloaf. After a few minutes, Dusty asked his mother if she knew where his clean shirts were.

She looked at him, puzzled. "Clean shirts? What are you talking about?"

"Well, tomorrow is picture day at school. I want to wear a nice shirt. Do you know where they are?" He looked hopefully at his mother, not realizing he had cornbread crumbs clinging to the corners of his mouth.

"Oh, baby. I guess I haven't done laundry in a while, have I?" With a heavy sigh, his mother stood up from the table and went into Dusty's bedroom. She came out with an armful of laundry a few moments later and dumped it on the kitchen floor.

"I'll wash some clothes tonight and we'll find something for you to wear in the morning, okay?" She sat at the table and rested her head in her hand.

"Okay, Mom. Thank you!" Dusty licked the chicken grease off his fingers and his lips.

"Dolores! I need another beer!" Earl was yelling from the living room.

"Get it yourself," she yelled back.

"C'mon, Dolores! You're right there. Get off your ass and bring me a beer!" He pounded his empty beer bottle on the side table.

"No! I've been working all day and I want to eat my dinner. Get your own damned beer!"

Dusty could see both adults from his seat at the kitchen table. His head swiveled back and forth between his mother and Earl, like they were in a tennis match.

"You're such a bitch!" There was a sudden sound of glass shattering as Earl threw the beer bottle against the wall. Earl made his way, on wobbly, drunken legs, into the kitchen. "Fine, you lazy cow, I'll get my own goddamn beer."

In a flash, Dusty's mother was out of her chair. "Get out! Get your ass out of my house," she was screaming at Earl, pointing her finger towards the front door. "And while you're at it, get a job, you useless piece of shit! All you've ever done is mooch off me. Well, not anymore. I'm tired of it! Get the hell out of here, once and for all!"

Dusty jumped from the kitchen chair and pressed his back against the refrigerator. It scared him when his mother yelled like this. If he could have, he would have run to his bedroom to hide, but Earl stood in the doorway to the hall, blocking the only way for Dusty to escape.

Still screaming at Earl, Dolores went into their bedroom and started throwing Earl's clothes into the small hallway. Dusty stood at attention, his eyes wide, as Earl and Dolores continued to argue.

"Aw, come on, Dolores. You don't mean that." Earl was gathering up the clothes from the floor almost as fast as Dolores was throwing them. "Wait a minute, Dolores. Let's talk this out. I've got nowhere to go. You can't just throw me out!"

With his arms loaded with clothes, Dolores pushed him out the door with her hands on the back of his shoulders. She grabbed his car keys that were hanging from a hook on the wall and threw them out the door, narrowly missing his head. She slammed the door and locked it before he could get back in. Dusty's mom had tossed Earl into the night.

Earl kept pounding on the door, begging her to let him back in, with promises to get a job. His pleading gave way to demands that she open the door right now and let him in, but Dolores didn't budge. She leaned her back against the door and covered her face with her hands. For every one of Earl's fists that pounded the door, Dolores's shoulders would jump. After a few minutes, Earl gave one last kick on the door and the pounding stopped. A moment later, Dolores heard the car door slam and the squeal of the tires as Earl drove away for the last time.

Slowly, Dusty walked into the living room. He could tell his mother was crying because her hands covered her face and her shoulders shook. He glided over to her and patted her arm. "It'll be okay, Mom. Please don't cry."

She sniffed, wiped her nose with the sleeve of her robe, and wrapped her arms around her son. "It's just you and me again, Dusty. Just you and me."

Dusty wrapped his arms around her waist and hugged her back. "That's okay, Mom. I like it better when it's just you and me."

"Me, too, baby. Me, too."

•   •   •   •   •

It would be another two years before Dolores got seriously involved with another man. Lloyd was the new chef at the Silver Dollar Diner and had just moved to the area after a recent divorce. He and Dolores seemed to hit it off, right from the beginning. He was smart, funny and best of all, he was not addicted to drugs or alcohol.

Lloyd and Dolores took it slowly at first, taking the time to get to know each other before going headlong into a serious relationship, both claiming they had been burned enough times before and did not want to get burned again.

Lloyd owned his own home, so he was not interested in moving in with Dolores and Dusty. He would occasionally stay overnight at Dolores' house, but would leave right after breakfast.

He also took an interest in Dusty, which something that none of her other boyfriends had ever done. Sometimes, when they were going out for dinner - Lloyd always paid - he would ask Dusty where he would like to go. It was a simple gesture, but Dolores noticed and was grateful for the attention Lloyd was giving her son.

They had been dating for about six months when Lloyd, Dolores, and Dusty drove to Atlantic City for a weekend. Dusty had never been on a vacation before and was excited to stay in a hotel for the very first time.

As they walked along the Boardwalk through the throngs of people, the three of them held hands to stay together. Dusty was so entranced by the sights and sounds at the pier that he wasn't watching where he was going. They had almost lost him twice after he wandered away from them, drawn to the flashing lights of the many marquees of the casinos.

When he saw the Ferris wheel, Dusty begged to be allowed to ride it. Dolores did not like heights so she said no, and truthfully, Lloyd didn't like heights either, but he gave in and bought two tickets - one for Dusty and one for him.

Lloyd kept his eyes closed and his hands tightly gripping the handlebar for the entire ride, unlike Dusty, who stretched over the bar to see as much as he could far below. He had the time of his life. He loved looking down from the very top of the ride and waving at his mother, whom he could barely see. She watched him lean over the handlebar and held her hand over her mouth, petrified that he might fall out.

Unfortunately for Dolores, her relationship with Lloyd would not last more than a few months past their trip. He had only accepted the job at the Silver Dollar Diner because it was the first job offer that came up when he moved to the area after his divorce. So, when Lloyd got a good job offer in Washington, D.C., he took it.

Dolores was heartbroken, but she understood. At first, they exchanged frequent phone calls after he moved away, but over time, those calls slowly diminished until they didn't talk at all. Time and distance was too much to overcome.

CHAPTER THREE

Dusty's mother, Dolores, was working second shift as a housekeeper at a local hotel. She didn't care for the late hours, but it paid more than the 9:00 AM-5:00 PM shift. Unfortunately, because of her late hours, she wasn't able to be a reliable presence for twelve-year-old Dusty like she had when he was younger. She would already be at work when he got home from school, and by the time she got home, it would be close to midnight. By then, Dusty would be asleep in bed.

Sometimes they would see each other on the weekends, but even that wasn't always the case. Dolores needed the money, so she tried to work as many extra hours as she could and that usually meant covering for other housekeepers who liked to have their weekends off.

As a single mother, she did the best that she could do, but she often wondered if it was enough. A child needs to be nurtured and cared for, taught lessons that no one but a parent could teach. A parent needs to spend time with their child, she knew.

Dolores tried to instill a sense of responsibility in her son. She would tell him he would need to pave his own way in this world and would need to do the very best he could do if he wanted to make something of himself. If he was smart, she would say, he wouldn't need to depend on anyone but himself.

Over the last eight years since Dusty's father had left them, Dolores tried to give Dusty what he needed, but life hadn't been easy for her. How could she teach Dusty to rise above, when the cards life had dealt her were always losing cards? Her life involved struggles, hurdles and fighting for every scrap she could get. She couldn't show him how to pull his ass out of the dumps when she herself had not been able to do it.

It would have been nice if Dusty had had a male role model, but that wasn't meant to be. She'd had men in her life, but none of them had lasted or been suitable role models for Dusty. They kept her bed warm at night, but that was about all they were good for. Most of the men she met were losers. Sometimes drunks, sometimes lazy and unemployed leeches, sometimes all the above.

She had complained to Dusty on multiple occasions that she wished things were different, that she couldn't even depend on his father for help. It was a bitter pill for her to swallow, but the day he left, he never looked back. In all this time, not once, she told Dusty, did he contact her for anything. Not once did he ever ask to spend time with Dusty. And not once did he ever send money to support her or his kid. She did not know where he was or what he was doing, she said. He could be dead for all she knew.

Dusty would complain to his mother that he didn't understand how his father could walk away from the family. She would simply tell him that maybe someday he would understand and then change the subject.

Despite her best wishes, about the only thing Dolores could teach Dusty was that life sucked.

•   •   •   •   •

Dusty missed spending time with his mother, although he wouldn't admit it openly. She had been the only parent he had known since he was a little kid, but he would not think about that. After all, he wasn't a baby anymore, and could take care of himself.

When Dusty got up in the morning, he would get himself ready for school, trying very hard to be quiet and not wake his mother. If she had remembered to go to the grocery store, there would be cereal for his breakfast. He would usually have to eat it dry, but on a good day, there would be milk. Most of the time, though, he would look in the cupboard, only to find it empty.

Without consistent parental guidance, it didn't take long before Dusty started having "behavioral" problems and getting into trouble at school. His teacher told his mother he was hanging out with the wrong crowd, but Dusty didn't see what was so wrong with his friends. They sure as hell weren't goody-two-shoes, but he and his buddies had fun.

Every few weeks, his mother would get a call from the teacher about his behavioral problems or his failing grades. When that happened, Dolores would give Dusty a good talking to. Sometimes, if she was in a bad mood, he would get grounded. She would tell him he wasn't allowed to hang out with his buddies after school, that he would have to come right home, stay home and do his homework. He didn't pay any attention to what his mother was telling him. It's not like she was home after he got out of school, anyway. She had no idea what he was doing, whether he was home or hanging out with his friends, so he just kept on doing what he wanted to do, and staying home to do his homework wasn't it.

Sometimes, Dusty and his pals would take lunch money from the younger, smaller kids. If the kid didn't give them money, they would get punched in the arm. Hard. Then the next time Dusty or his buddies asked for money, the kid would usually give it up, preferring to go hungry rather than get punched.

Dusty and his friends were getting pretty good at stealing things from the stores without getting caught. However, the first time they were apprehended, Target security had spotted Dusty and three of his friends stuffing Yu-Gi-Oh cards into their pockets. A couple of his buddies ran off, but loss prevention caught two of them, and Dusty was one of those two.

The police were called, but because they were juveniles and it was a petty crime, all the cop could do was lecture Dusty and his accomplice, Nehemiah. The cop tried to scare them by telling them they were breaking the law by shoplifting, that if they weren't careful, they could be arrested and sent to Juvenile Hall. Dusty wasn't scared. He figured they wouldn't send him to Juvie for stealing little things like Yu-Gi-Oh cards and candy bars, so he kept right on taking what didn't belong to him. Occasionally, he would get caught, but nothing ever happened, and it didn't matter to him, anyway. After all, why should he stop stealing when nothing would ever be done about it?

·　　·　　·　　·　　·

Dusty was thirteen when he tried marijuana for the first time. He would not admit it to his buddies, but he didn't care for it. Pot made him hungry, and Dusty didn't like being hungry all the time. His buddies would laugh about it, calling the effect "getting the munchies" but then they would either go home to eat dinner with their families or they would steal things to eat, like chips and Slim Jim meat sticks. But for Dusty, it wasn't that easy. He knew there wasn't enough food at home, so that left him with two choices... he could either stay hungry or he could continue to steal things like food with his friends.

The only good part of getting high was that he enjoyed laughing over silly stuff that normally wouldn't be funny at all. At least when he was laughing, he wasn't thinking about his stomach growling.

Dolores had found a pot pipe in his jeans pocket one day when she was sorting the clothes for laundry. She waved it in his face and yelled at him.

"What is this? Are you smoking pot with your derelict friends?"

"Pfftt, what do you mean 'derelict friends'? My friends aren't like that and you've got no right judging them." Dusty stood defiantly in front of his mother, his hands crossed in front of his chest, his head tipped to the side.

Her yelling got louder until she was screaming at him. "How many times have I told you to be responsible? To act like a man? How many times have I told you I don't want drugs in this house?"

Before either of them knew what had happened, Dolores raised her hand and slapped Dusty across the face.

For a moment, they both stared at each other, neither one saying a word. She had never hit him before. He put his hand on his cheek, his eyes reading surprise and then anger.

"Oh, my God. Dusty, I'm sorry. I'm so sorry, baby…" She reached out to touch his face, where a red imprint of her hand was already showing.

Before she could reach him, he turned and ran out the door. As he took off down the road, he felt a single tear fall, leaving a wet trail across the sting on his cheek.

•　　•　　•　　•　　•

By the time Dusty was sixteen, he had dropped out of school, choosing instead to hang out on the streets. He was smoking weed daily and had graduated to alcohol as well. There were enough older kids around or even the occasional adult who would be willing to buy a bottle for Dusty, as long as he gave them a couple of bucks for their trouble. It wasn't unusual to find Dusty either stoned, drunk, or both, every single day.

However, with no steady source of income, he was quickly turning to a life of crime to support the ever-increasing need for a high. The only way he knew to raise money was to steal, since he had no interest in getting a job. He would steal whatever he could, anything from video games to steaks, and then sell it for a percentage of its value to any number of acquaintances on the street. He'd been doing it for long enough that he had learned what items to steal based on what was in demand and who would be willing to pay top dollar.

It didn't take Dusty long to realize that, when it came to larceny, it was quantity vs. quality. Small items didn't get him as much money, but he could usually get away with stealing more of those smaller items at once. Larger items and more expensive and in-demand items were harder to steal, so he could get more money for them. However, with those high-priced items came a greater risk of getting caught. Dusty didn't care about the risk, as long as he made enough cash to buy his pot and his booze.

Finally, after coming home drunk one night, Dusty's mother had had enough and told him he wasn't to come home at all if he was under the influence of drugs or alcohol. She was kicking him out.

Dusty's eyes were wide open with disbelief. "Mom, you can't do that. I live here!"

"I don't care, Dusty. You won't listen to me, but I've told you over and over again. I've had enough men in my life over the years who were drunks or drug addicts, and I will not take that kind of shit from my own son."

"This is bullshit. Where am I supposed to go?" He swayed, one hand holding onto a kitchen chair for balance, as he looked at his mother through red, bleary eyes.

"That's up to you. As long as you keep getting high, you're not staying here." She pointed at Dusty with the ever-present cigarette dangling between her two fingers. "If you get rid of the weed, the alcohol, and anything else you're on, you can come back, but not until you straighten your ass out."

Dusty turned and headed out the front door. He slammed the door closed as he left. If he had looked back at his mother, he would have seen the tears streaming down her face as her legs gave way and she collapsed onto the sofa. He was in no shape to understand how difficult it was for her to throw him out.

From that point on, Dusty floated from one place to the next. Sometimes he would crash on a friend's couch when the parents took pity on him. He would lie to them and say that his mother was the problem, that she was an abusive alcoholic and had kicked him out. Sometimes he would say that there was always a steady line of men parading through the front door, right into her bedroom. Whatever he thought would garner the most sympathy is what he told them.

Unfortunately for Dusty, the results were always the same. After four or five days, the friend's parents would realize that Dusty was nothing but trouble. They would smell the alcohol on his breath or the weed on his clothes. Sometimes, they would discover that money was missing from their wallets, purses and piggy banks. He had even gotten caught stealing a pair of earrings from a friend's mother. Eventually, the parents would see first-hand the influence and negative impact Dusty had on their own kids as they tried to emulate Dusty's behavior. Time after time, he would end up back on the streets.

The lack of parental guidance and the fact that his time was his own was taking its toll on young Dusty.

He had no structure, no rules, and no role model. Like so many addicts, getting high became his escape and the only thing he cared about.

· · · · ·

When Dusty was seventeen and his friend Nehemiah was eighteen, they stole a car. They had been hanging out in front of a mom-and-pop grocery store, passing time by watching traffic and people pass by. A middle-aged man, obviously in a hurry, had left his car running in the parking lot and dashed into the store. Dusty and Nehemiah looked at the car and then looked back at each other. Neither one said a word as they both broke into grins, reading each other's mind.

They sprinted towards the car, a fairly new Infiniti Q50. Nehemiah jumped into the driver's seat while Dusty, laughing, fell into the passenger seat. Nehemiah squealed the tires as he maneuvered the stolen car into traffic, just missing the back end of a passing pickup truck. At the sound of squealing tires and the horn blasting from the truck, the car's owner rushed out of the store. He yelled for them to stop, but was forced to watch in shock as Nehemiah kept driving.

"This is freaking awesome, man!" Dusty said, laughing. He pounded on the glove box like he was playing the drums in a heavy metal band.

"Let's see how fast this baby can go!" Nehemiah wove in and out of traffic, taking the route that would lead them out of town and away from other vehicles. He pressed on the gas pedal, forcing the car to go faster and faster along the country roads, until he was traveling at 100 mph for several miles on an open stretch of road. The only other vehicle they saw was a slow-moving farm tractor pulling a large wagon filled with freshly baled hay. Nehemiah sailed past the tractor like it was standing still. The farmer, startled, blasted the horn. Dusty and Nehemiah laughed as Nehemiah pressed on the Infiniti's horn to return the favor. Dusty pumped his fist in the air through the open sunroof.

"Woo whoo!" Nehemiah cheered. "This is an awesome car!"

The sudden wail of a siren coming from behind them drowned out his voice. Nehemiah looked in the rear view mirror; Dusty looked over his left shoulder. On their back bumper, with lights and siren blazing, was a Maryland State Police officer. The farmer pulling the hay wagon had called 9-1-1 from his cell phone.

"Shit," said Nehemiah. "It's the cops!"

"Keep going! Don't let them catch us, man!" Dusty yelled.

"Are you kidding? There's no way I can outrun him. I gotta pull over." Nehemiah pulled to the side of the road, gently pressing on the brake to slow the car. Given the speed they'd been going, it was a good quarter mile before the car coasted to a complete stop. The State Police car stopped right behind them.

The trooper stayed in his car, but used the loudspeaker on his car radio to give Dusty and Nehemiah directions. "Stay in the car and do not make any sudden moves. I need you to follow my directions. Driver, put your hands on the steering wheel." Nehemiah did as he was told.

"Passenger, put your hands on the dashboard." Dusty obeyed. "Don't move. Just stay as you are," the officer commanded.

They waited in silence for a couple of minutes until three more State Police officers joined them and stopped their vehicles around the stolen Infiniti. The troopers exited their cars with guns drawn and positioned themselves behind their cars, facing Nehemiah and Dusty.

The initial trooper resumed giving them orders. "Driver, keep your right hand on the steering wheel, and with your left hand, roll down the side windows, yours and the passenger's." Nehemiah pressed the buttons on the armrest to roll down the windows. "Driver, reach out of the window with your left hand and grab the door handle on the outside of the car... Open the door." Nehemiah instinctively reached for the inside door handle, then realized what the trooper had told him, and quickly reached for the handle outside the car. He slowly opened the door.

"Driver," continued the trooper, "slowly step out of the vehicle... Face forward... Now put your hands behind your head and interlock your fingers... Step backwards to the sound of my voice until I tell you to stop... Stop... Driver, get on your knees... Driver, lay down on your stomach with your arms extended all the way out." Nehemiah laid down, resting his chin on the pavement. From behind him, he heard the sound of footsteps approaching. His hands were yanked behind him, first one and then the other, and he heard the click of metal as a trooper placed the handcuffs on his wrists. He expected to be allowed to get up, but was left laying on the roadway. The trooper went back to his car, taking cover behind it.

"Passenger, I need you to follow my directions. Reach with your right hand and grab the door handle on the outside of the car... Open the door... Slowly step out of the vehicle." The trooper ran through the same steps that he had given Nehemiah.

Once Dusty was on the ground and handcuffed, they were both lifted to a standing position, patted down for weapons, and then placed in the back of two different trooper cars. Dusty hung his head. He'd been in trouble before, but nothing like this. His mother was going to kill him.

•   •   •   •   •

Dusty spent five weeks in jail waiting for his case to be resolved. His court-appointed attorney had struck a deal where Dusty would plead to the misdemeanor charge of unauthorized use of a motor vehicle and would be given time served. Because he was the passenger, and because he'd had nothing but a couple of petty theft charges as a juvenile, the district attorney went easy on him.

The judge, however, gave him a stern talking to and told him he was traveling down the wrong road. "It doesn't have to be like this. You can make something of your life and make your mother proud." At the judge's words, Dusty looked over his shoulder. His mother was sitting in the front row, looking at him with the saddest eyes he'd ever seen. His chest clenched at the sight. It never occurred to him he was hurting her with his actions. He looked back at the judge, but he'd stopped listening. His mind was on his mother. He didn't think he would ever forget the look of disappointment on her face.

Before Dusty was released from jail later that day, he said goodbye to Nehemiah. It would be the last time Dusty would ever see him.

The judge had sentenced Nehemiah to six months in jail for auto theft since he was the driver and because he had been arrested once before for the same crime.

Months later, after Nehemiah had been released from jail, he was found dead from an overdose of heroin. He had been out of jail for only a week.

Chapter Four

Two years had passed. Dusty Sampson was sitting at the kitchen table in his mother's house. Dust motes, visible in the sunlight that was streaming through the window, danced in the air above his head. Dolores was talking to him, but he kept his head down and picked at a hangnail on his thumb. He couldn't bear to look at her. He had just been released from jail after spending eight months behind bars for possession of narcotics. His mother was establishing the terms by which she would allow him to live with her.

"Listen, Dusty. I know you've got nowhere else to go, so you can stay here with me, but you're going to have to get a job and stay sober. You did great getting sober in jail, but now you have to stay that way. You know I don't like drugs and I don't want that shit in my house."

Dolores waited for him to say something. "Dusty, do you hear me?"

"Yeah, Ma. I hear you." Dusty stood up, the chair making a scraping noise on the worn linoleum, and walked into the living room. Dolores watched as

Dusty stopped in front of the large picture window that overlooked the front yard. His warm breath fogged the glass, making it difficult to see past the glass, but he didn't seem to notice.

Dolores came up from behind him and put her hand on his shoulder. "I know you can do this, Dusty. You don't need to live the life of a drug addict. Don't you see? You were doing so well in prison. You got clean and sober, and you started working on your GED. Those are good things, Dusty. You can do this. I know you can." She gave his shoulder a supportive squeeze.

"Whatever," was all he said before he shook her hand free and walked out the front door. Dolores watched from the door as he walked down the sidewalk, his eyes downcast, his hands in his pockets. She quietly closed the door.

Three days later, Dolores was stirring tomato soup on the kitchen stove when she heard the front door open. She hoped Dusty would have some good news. When she looked at him over her shoulder, she saw him smiling at her, so she returned the smile.

"You look happy. Do you have good news?"

"I got a job. Can you believe it?" Dusty was grinning and as she looked at her son, Dolores realized it had been a long time since she'd seen him smile.

"Oh, Dusty, that's fantastic! I knew you could do this! I'm so proud of you." She turned to give him a hug, the spoon still in her hand. Drops of tomato soup landed on the floor behind Dusty. He hugged her back for the first time in a long while. Dolores took a step back, keeping her hands on his shoulders, and said, "Let's go out. Let's go to dinner somewhere to celebrate. I'll let you pick the place."

"No, Ma, we don't need to do that. It's just a job. No big deal." Dolores could see that although his voice said no, his smile said yes.

"I don't want to hear any arguments. We're going." She turned off the burner, the decision made.

They decided to go to Froggy's Bar and Grill for pizza and wings. They both ordered a draft beer while they waited for their food.

"So, tell me about the job. What will you be doing?"

"It's really not a big deal, Ma. I'm just a dishwasher at the Cracker Barrel."

"Well, you might not think it's a big deal, but I do. Any job is a good job, Dusty, and you have to start somewhere, right? Who knows? You might be a dishwasher today, but maybe in a couple of months, you can move up to food prep and then someday you might be a famous chef like they have on television. Sometimes, one thing will lead to another and lead you down a road you didn't think you'd be on."

"Yeah, I guess so. We'll see." The server brought their beers, and had barely set the glass down in front of Dusty before he grabbed it and took a long swig, almost finishing the beer.

"That tasted good," Dusty said as he wiped the foam from his top lip with the back of his hand. "I haven't had a beer in over eight months."

Dolores looked on with concern. "Be careful, Dusty. A beer once in a while is okay, but don't go crazy."

"Don't worry about it. I can handle it." Dusty gave his mother a dirty look and finished the beer in one large gulp. He slammed the empty glass on the table, harder than he needed to. Dolores knew better than to say anything, but was visibly concerned when Dusty flagged down a passing server and ordered another beer.

. . . . .

A month later, Dolores sat in the living room of her home, watching the evening news on TV. She heard someone fumbling with the doorknob. She turned to face the front door and, for a moment, held her breath, afraid that someone was trying to break in. To her relief, Dusty walked in. Or, more appropriately, he fell in.

"Oh, my god, Dusty. You scared the shit out of me." Her good-natured smile quickly disappeared when she saw the condition he was in.

"Why would I scare the shit out of you? Iss juss me. I'm not that ugly." His lip curled into a crooked smile. "Hey, you got anythin' to eat around here?" Dusty stood in front of his mother, weaving from side to side as if he was on a ship. He tipped too far to the right but caught himself on the wall before he fell to the floor. He stayed like that, with one shoulder leaning against the wall to steady himself.

"What is the matter with you?" Dolores snuffed out her lipstick-rimmed cigarette in the ashtray without watching what she was doing, and knocked a few crumpled butts and ashes onto the coffee table. "What the hell have you done to yourself, Dusty? And why are you home? You are supposed to be at work."

"Ah, screw that. I quit that job. It was making my hands look like prunes." Dusty started laughing, as if it was the funniest thing he'd heard all day.

"Are you serious? What is wrong with you? Dusty, are you high or something?"

"Nah, I juss had a couple beers with Shit Storm."

"Shit Storm?" Dolores repeated. "What kind of name is that?"

"Shit Storm McCracken. His real name is Seamus McCracken, but he doesn't like the name Seamus, so everyone just calls him Shit Storm. He's a guy I met in pris'n. Iss okay, Ma. He's a nice guy."

"Uh, huh. And you quit your job?" Dolores folded her arms across her chest and glared at Dusty. She was clearly angry.

"Iss no big deal, Ma. I'll get another job. Iss juss that the boss at Cracker Barrel is a real asshole. He didn't like it that I was late a couple of times. But I sure fixed his ass. I quit." Dusty, still leaning against the wall, looked at his mother. The corners of his mouth lifted into a lopsided grin.

Dolores stood in front of her son with a look of disappointment. "Oh, God, Dusty. Look at you! You're a mess! I told you, if you wanted to live here, you had to stay clean and sober, and get a job. That's all I asked. Why is that so hard?"

"C'mon, Ma. Don't be such a bitch. I'm telling you, I'll get another job. Iss not a big deal."

Dolores dropped her arms to her side and stood as tall as her 5'4" frame would allow. "What did you just call me?"

"Pfft. Whatever." Dusty walked past his mother and headed towards his bedroom. She could hear the creak of his bed frame as he fell onto the bed.

· · · · ·

Dusty woke up the next morning, still in the clothes he wore the night before. He had a splitting headache and his stomach hurt like hell. His tongue felt like someone had run over it and left it on the pavement to dry. As he forced himself to sit up, the room began to spin. He had to take a couple of deep breaths to stop himself from retching. It had been a long time since he'd felt this badly.

As he sat on the edge of the bed, he ran his fingers through his hair, but even that hurt. What in the hell happened? Slowly, the events from the night before began to take shape in his cloudy memory. He remembered telling his boss that he had quit. The next memory that came into focus was sitting in McCracken's car on the way to Froggy's Bar and Grill. But how he hooked up with McCracken, he couldn't remember. Did he call him for a ride? Maybe. Who knows?

He recalled doing shots with McCracken at Froggy's, but that's the last thing he remembered. Slowly, so as not to jar his brain, he looked around at the familiar surroundings, and realized he was home, in his own bedroom. He had no clue how he got there.

Dusty carefully and slowly stood up. The room was spinning, making it hard to stand and even harder to avoid puking. Holding his hand over his mouth, Dusty ran towards the bathroom. He knelt down on the floor and emptied the contents of his stomach into the toilet. He heaved until there was nothing left. Once he was done, he leaned back on his heels, with his hands wrapped around the toilet seat. He laid his head on his arms. hugging the toilet.

A voice came from the doorway behind him. "Look at you. You're a mess. Why did you do it, Dusty? Why did you have to get so drunk? You'd been doing so good, and now look at you."

"Yeah, I know, Ma. I don't need you telling me that. Man, I feel like shit."

"Don't come crying to me because I don't want to hear it. I should throw your ass out, Dusty. I told you, I don't want you coming home like this. No more drugs; no more drunkenness. That was the deal. And you need to have a job." Dolores paused and looked at her son. "I shouldn't do this, but I'm going to give you one more chance. I shouldn't, but I will. So help me, Dusty, if it happens again, you're done. Do you understand me?"

Dolores didn't wait for a reply. She left her son in a heap on the bathroom floor as she turned on her heel, stormed to her bedroom, and slammed the door, the noise reverberating in Dusty's head.

CHAPTER FIVE

Dusty had been bouncing from job to job, washing dishes in one restaurant or another for about a year. For the last two months, he'd been out of work after being fired yet again. He'd told his mother that he was trying to find a job, that no one was hiring. He was lying to her. He wasn't even looking.

He'd fallen into his old habits with his old friends, and was drunk and high almost every hour of every day. More often than not, he would come home late at night, swaying when he stood in front of her, his glassy eyes unable to focus as he made his way to his bedroom, ricocheting off the walls until he finally landed in bed.

He had tried to hide it from his mother, but she had seen right through the stories he'd concocted. It won't happen again, he'd say. He wasn't stoned, just tired. Or, his eyes were red from allergies. Or, it was the first time in a long time, so he was entitled to let his hair down once in a while.

Still, Dolores didn't want to give up on Dusty. She tried repeatedly to reason with him, but her pleas fell on deaf ears. She was well-aware of the ultimatum she had given him, and finally, she'd had enough. She tossed his ass out of her house, leaving him to fend for himself. He ended up crashing on whatever couch with whatever friends he could find.

Luckily for Dusty, he'd been able to stay in Rockville with his friend Jorge Ortega and Jorge's girlfriend, Maria Castellano, for the last couple of months. They had known each other for several years, ever since they had gone to junior high school together. They had lost contact after high school but had reconnected a couple of years ago while Dusty was working as a dishwasher and Jorge had been a bartender at the same restaurant.

When he didn't have cash for rent, Dusty would steal cigarettes, food, makeup, or whatever he could get his hands on, and they would take that as payment for letting him stay on their couch. They did not condone Dusty's stealing, but they were not in a financial position to where they could turn down the "gifts" that he offered them. Jorge and Maria simply looked the other way and did not ask Dusty where he was getting these random items. After all, if they didn't ask, they wouldn't know, and if they didn't know, they couldn't judge.

·   ·   ·   ·   ·

Dusty paced back and forth in the living room of Maria's house like a caged animal. He was trying to figure out a plan to get some cash. The situation was getting critical. He had been without money for a while now, and was racking up some sizable IOUs. His friends' generosity would last only so long. Even McCracken was losing patience with Dusty's lack of funds. Dusty knew he needed money, and he needed it quickly.

If he got a job today, it would still be another couple of weeks before he got a paycheck. There had to be a better way to get his hands on some quick cash. Dusty stopped his pacing and stood in front of the large picture window behind the couch, his arms crossed in front of his chest. His eyes looked without seeing, his mind lost in thought. He rubbed his temples, as if the calming touch would help him formulate a plan.

The view out the picture window was the same one he'd seen a thousand times. It was the front of Habibi's Middle Eastern Market, the store window cluttered with decals advertising cigarettes, vaping supplies and hot gyros. He watched a woman with a plastic grocery bag come out as a man entered the store. Then it came to him; he could rob a store. *Habibi's always had tons of people going into the store every single day. They must have a lot of cash on hand.*

Dusty began pacing again, running his hands through his hair, as he thought about his idea. By robbing a store, he could get the money he wanted. But what store could he rob? Definitely not Habibi's because they would recognize him. He was in and out of that store a couple of times a week. It would have to be a store nearby, though. He would have to find a store within walking distance, say a couple of blocks, since he didn't have a car. And it would have to be a store that he never went into so they wouldn't recognize him.

He knew of one store - he didn't know the name, but it was a small mom-and-pop place - where an older couple tended the store. *I've been in there once or twice,* Dusty thought, *but they probably wouldn't recognize me since I haven't gone there in two or three months. And an older couple like that would be easy to steal from. It's not like they would put up a fight.* The more he thought about it, the more he liked that idea.

He decided he would need a mask to make sure no one recognized him. Often, he would see Maria with a red bandana that she had rolled up and wrapped around her head to pull her hair back. He could use that to cover his face like they did in the old-time cops and robber movies.

Dusty ran upstairs to the bathroom, where Maria had a drawer full of hair brushes, scrunchies and barrettes. In that same drawer, Dusty found the bandana he was looking for.

He unrolled it, put it over his nose and mouth, and tied it in the back. Dusty looked at himself in the bathroom mirror and liked what he saw. There's no way the old couple would ever know it was him.

He could smell Maria's shampoo on the bandana and, for a moment, he wondered if he should go through with his plan to rob the store. Maria and Jorge were his friends and would probably be disappointed in him if they knew. He'd stolen so much in the past that he couldn't begin to count how many times he'd done it. And he also knew that stealing something from a shelf wasn't the same as forcing someone to hand over the cash from the till. Dusty knew that was the difference between larceny and robbery.

Then again, desperate times called for desperate measures, and he would just have to make sure Jorge and Maria didn't find out. He would keep his mouth shut and they would never know.

That same afternoon, Dusty left the house with the bandana tied around his neck. For now, he let it hang below his chin. He walked through the back alleys until he got to the store.

Standing at the corner of the building for a few moments, he watched as customers went in, and then made sure they came back out again. He didn't want anyone to be in the store, other than the older couple. When the last customer that had gone in had come back out again, Dusty knew it was time to make his move.

His heart was racing, the sound of his heartbeat thrumming in his ears. He took a deep breath and, with one hand on the doorknob, he lifted the bandana to cover his face. As he pulled open the door with his left hand, he put his right hand in the pocket of his sweatshirt and held his finger straight out. He wanted to make it look like he had a gun in his pocket.

"Give me all your money! Give it to me now!" Dusty yelled at the old man, who stood behind the counter. The man threw both hands in the air.

"Open the register, old man, and give me the money!" Dusty pushed his "gun" finger towards the man. The man looked at Dusty's pocket and quickly hit a button on the cash register. The drawer popped open, and the man stepped back, his hands in the air once again.

"Take the money. I don't want no trouble," the old man said with an accent. Dusty reached over the counter and grabbed as many bills as he could from each compartment in the till. He spun on his heel and darted out the door. He was in and out of the store in less than a minute.

What Dusty didn't know is that the old man had seen Dusty just outside the door as he lifted the bandana to his face. The old man had one finger on the silent alarm button, just in case. The moment Dusty came in yelling for the money, the old man pushed the alarm button and then put his hands in the air. The police were on their way.

Dusty ran through the alleys and was a block from home when he heard the sirens. He ran faster until he was up the steps and through the front door. He turned and locked the door behind him.

He paced the length of the living room, a feeling of exhilaration competing with a sense of nervousness. He let out a maniacal laugh and pumped the air with his fist. Almost as an afterthought, he reached into the pocket of his sweatshirt and pulled out the cash.

It was then that he realized he had reached for the cash in the register and put what cash he had grabbed into his sweatshirt pocket, all with his right hand. The same hand that he had concealed in the pocket of his sweatshirt to make it look like a gun.

Dusty closed his eyes, thankful that the old man hadn't realized there was no gun. It could have been a problem if the old man had put up a fight.

With a shake of his head, Dusty sat on the couch and began counting his take, laying the twenty's, tens, fives and ones in their own piles. It was easier for him to count it that way. He counted out $324 that he had stolen from the store. He laughed harder.

· · · · ·

The next day, Dusty gave Jorge and Maria $100 cash. Maria raised her eyebrows questioningly, but Dusty just smiled.

"I won the lottery," he told her.

She looked at the money in her hand and said simply, "Thanks, Dusty."

For the next week, Dusty went on a buying spree. He bought marijuana and whiskey for himself and

McCracken. He filled up the gas tank for McCracken twice and bought pizza and wings for Jorge and Maria. And he stopped by his mother's house, with a bouquet of fresh flowers.

"Are you working, Dusty? Did you get a job?" She smiled at her son.

"No, not yet, Mom, but I'm working on it." Dolores gave Dusty a sideways glance, wondering what he was up to, but she didn't ask because she didn't want to know.

· · · · ·

It wasn't long before Dusty ran out of money. He looked in his wallet and found he had just $3 left. It wasn't enough to buy even a cheap bottle of whiskey or a couple bags of pot. It was then that he realized, with a sinking feeling, he was right back where he started from. He felt like someone had punched him in the gut.

He couldn't believe the money was all gone. He was going to have to come up with another plan to get even more cash. What he'd gotten from the small grocery store was nice, but obviously wasn't enough. He would need to get more money.

He decided to rob some place bigger. The bigger the place, he figured, the more money they would have. That's when the idea came to him to rob a restaurant where he used to work, and that restaurant was Rosalee's Restaurant. The food was good there, and they were always crowded. Surely they would have a lot of cash on hand.

Dusty had lasted longer at Rosalee's than he had at most of his other jobs - probably about six months - and was familiar with their routine. He thought about the logistics of robbing the restaurant and finally came up with a plan. He decided that it would be best to rob them at closing time when they would have the most cash on hand and there wouldn't be any customers who could get in the way. Dusty would go in, demand that they open the safe where they kept the cash, and give it all to him.

In order to do it right, he would need to use Maria's bandana again. But he was concerned about keeping the bandana for too long. What if she went looking for it? How could he ever explain that it was in his possession? The bandana had to be put back.

He could always get another bandana or even a ski mask so the employees at Rosalee's wouldn't recognize him, but that was easy to get. He could easily buy something - or rather, steal something - from Walmart.

He would need transportation, not only to get to the restaurant but also to get the hell out of there after the robbery, so he had to figure out how he was going to get wheels. The best way would be to borrow a car from someone, but none of his friends ever lent him their cars, knowing he was too drunk or drugged to drive on any given day or night. The state had also suspended his license after he received a couple of speeding tickets and never answered them, and some of his friends were aware of that as well. They were not willing to risk having their cars wrecked or towed because of Dusty.

He'd tried calling a couple of people anyway to see if they would let him borrow their car but they all said no. No surprise there. He would have no choice but to ask someone if they could give him a ride, although that would have to be done carefully. If he explained what he was doing, no one would want to be a part of it. His best bet was Shit Storm McCracken.

Dusty sent a text message to McCracken. "Dude, I need a ride Friday night. You up for it?"

A few minutes later, Dusty got a response. "Its gonna cost you. I told you. No more free rides."

"I'll give you a hundred," Dusty typed back.

"Where you get that kinda paper?"

"Doing a deal. That's all you need to know."

"Fine. What time?"

"Imma need to be at Rosalee's at 1 AM."

"I be at your place at 1230."

Now that he had the ride arranged, the next thing he would need to work on was getting a gun. The restaurant manager, Mike something or other, was a nice guy and probably wouldn't put up a fight, but Dusty wasn't taking any chances. With a gun, they would know he wasn't kidding around, that he meant business. Having a real gun would also work better than using his finger.

The problem was how he was going to get his hands on a gun. He knew a woman, Amy Hoffman, who used to sell him drugs. She had a nephew that used to deal with all kinds of things, including guns. Although he didn't know the nephew that well, Dusty figured it might be worth getting in touch with Amy to see if she would relay his messages to her nephew. He and Amy were friends on Facebook, so he could send her a message.

Since his burner phone didn't have access to the web, Maria had been letting Dusty use her laptop while he was staying with them. He grabbed the computer from the kitchen counter and brought it to the couch. He signed into his Facebook account, opened up Messenger, and quickly searched for Amy's name.

"Hey, I need a favor," he wrote.

She answered right away. "What's up?"

"Your kin still able to get things?"

"Depends. What you need?"

"Imma need some heat." Dusty was using slang, but he knew Amy would understand what he meant.

"It'll cost you."

"I know that. I gotta have certain things to complete a job."

"I'll let you know."

Over the next few days, Amy and Dusty messaged back and forth until they struck a deal. From the proceeds of the robbery, Dusty would give Amy $200 for acting as the go-between for Dusty and her nephew, Vince Gardner. Vince insisted on getting paid $300 for the gun, with the proviso that Dusty return the firearm within forty-eight hours. It would not be his to keep. Renting the gun to his street-thug friends had become a lucrative business for Vince, and he told his aunt he wasn't about to lose an opportunity that might come up if Dusty kept the gun any longer than was necessary. To make his point, Vince threatened Dusty with physical harm if he did not return the gun on time. Dusty readily agreed to have the gun back in Vince's hands before the forty-eight hours were up.

Vince had wanted to meet with Dusty at Amy's house to exchange the weapon. She lived about a mile away from where Dusty was staying, but Vince wouldn't have it any other way since he and Dusty didn't know each other. Amy agreed they could meet at her house.

On Thursday evening, Dusty set out at a fast pace and walked to Amy's. He had a lot riding on this meeting with Vince and he was anxious to get to it. The air was chilly for a fall evening in Maryland, but he failed to notice the cold on his bare arms. He was too focused on the pending gun exchange to pay attention to the weather.

As soon as he got to Amy's house, Dusty ran up the wooden porch steps and banged on the screen door with a closed fist. From inside, he heard a voice telling him to "come in." He let himself in, flinching as the screen door slammed behind him. His nerves were on edge.

An obese woman sat up on a hospital bed within sight of the front door. What would normally be a living room had been renovated into Amy's bedroom. At almost 450 pounds, she spent most of her time in the bed. "Hey, Dusty. You're right on time. I like that. How about a treat? It's on the house."

With his eyes wide, Dusty eyed the heroin that was on a small table next to the bed. "No, man. I can't. I gotta stay focused."

"You sure?" she prodded. "It's on the house."

"No way. Like I said, I gotta stay focused." Dusty frowned at Amy and nervously waved his hand in the air. "Don't try to derail my plans."

"That's cool. I'm not trying to bust your plans. No worries." Amy reached over and grabbed a doughnut from a box that sat right next to the heroin.

As they waited for Vince to bring the gun, Dusty paced in what little space there was, between the foot of the hospital bed and a dresser. A television, tuned to *Wheel of Fortune,* rested on top of the dresser. Amy tried to make small talk, but Dusty was too apprehensive to offer much more than one- or two-word answers.

After a half-hour, Vince still hadn't arrived with the gun. "Man, you gotta ask the dude where in hell he's at. I'm not waiting all night."

"Relax, will ya? Why don't you just chill out and I'll see if I can get a hold of him." Amy reached for the laptop that rested on the bed next to her. Dusty watched her type something as he nervously chewed on his thumbnail.

After a few minutes, Amy said, "Vince said he can't make it tonight. He'll be here tomorrow morning." She closed the lid on the laptop.

"Are you kidding me?" Dusty was angry. He did not want his plans to fall through now. He was too close to seeing them come to fruition. "That's bullshit!"

"He said he'll be here at 10:00 tomorrow morning," Amy repeated. "He promises."

"He damn-well better be." Dusty turned and stomped out the door, purposely slamming the screen door on his way.

· · · · ·

After a restless night with very little sleep, Dusty walked back to Amy's house the next morning. Vince was already there by the time Dusty arrived a few minutes after 10:00.

Vince held the gun in front of Dusty, but pulled it back as Dusty reached for it. "Forty-eight hours, man. That's all you got. I want the gun back in my hands by then. You got that?" Vince firmly poked Dusty in the chest with his finger. "And it'll run you $300 cash. Normally I get paid up front, but since my Aunt Amy is vouching for you, I'll let it slide, but just this once."

Dusty, without taking his eyes off the gun, answered, "Yeah, I hear you. I'll meet you back here Sunday morning with the money and the gun."

Vince put the promised gun, a Luger Hi-Point 9mm semi-automatic handgun, into Dusty's hand. Dusty felt the heft of the gun, gently tossing it up and down in his hand. He noticed someone had filed off the serial number and smiled. He then tucked it in his waistband, carefully pulling his shirt over the weapon. Dusty left Amy's house feeling relieved that his plans were beginning to come together.

When Dusty got home, he saw that Jorge and Maria were in the kitchen having lunch. He offered a quick "hello" and then dashed upstairs to the bathroom. He pulled the gun out of his waistband and smiled as he studied it. As he stood in front of the mirror over the sink, he practiced aiming at his reflection, acting as if he was shooting it. The weapon gave him a newfound feeling of confidence and power. He liked that.

With a satisfied smile, Dusty pumped the air with his fist. His plans were made and in place. All he had to do now was wait for McCracken to show up at 12:30 that night, about thirteen hours away.

· · · · ·

Friday evening had finally arrived, but Dusty was feeling the pressure after waiting around all day for the minutes to tick by. He took a few hits of marijuana, trying to relax. Unfortunately, his mind couldn't be quieted, and he started getting anxious when he did the math and realized that a major chunk of money would go to Amy and Vince. *What if there isn't much cash in the safe tonight? After paying them $500, how much would it leave for me? And I have to pay Shit Storm $100 for the ride, also.*

Dusty decided that the only thing better than robbing a restaurant on a Friday night was robbing another one on Saturday. That way, he figured he could get even more money and would be sitting pretty. If he had enough money left after settling the debts with Amy, Vince, and McCracken, he might even be able to take off and go somewhere to lie low for a while.

He remembered the summer when he was a young kid that Dusty, his mother, and one of her boyfriends had gone to Atlantic City. It was the only time he'd ever gone away on vacation - let alone out of state - and he'd never forgotten how the lights, sights, and sounds of the tourist town amazed him. Maybe he could hang out there for a while. Yes. That sounded like a damn good idea. That's what he would do.

He reached for the laptop and started messaging Amy. "Imma do another deal tomorrow night. That's better than doing just one job tonight."

"I don't care what you do. Just make sure you bring Vince his thing on Sunday morning. He serious."

"I know." Dusty shook his head. He wasn't in any kind of mood to listen to Amy's lectures.

He'd have to talk to McCracken tonight and make sure he'd be able to give him a ride tomorrow night as well. But after robbing Rosalee's, he'd have enough money to entice McCracken, two nights in a row. That should work. He needed to think about which place to rob next, though.

The marijuana and the lack of sleep from the night before were catching up to Dusty. He laid down on the couch and closed his eyes, hoping to take a nap for a couple of hours. After he slept for a bit, he'd figure out what place to rob the next night.

CHAPTER SIX

Natalie Petrenko and David Hamlin had been working together at Rosalee's Restaurant for the last two years, David as a cook and Natalie as a server. David had started a few months before Natalie, but the minute she came through the door, it was love at first sight. They'd been a couple ever since.

They spent as much time together as they could, thoroughly enjoying each other's company. David was a kind person, who had a knack for making Natalie laugh. Natalie loved watching David cook, and was a willing guinea pig when he wanted to try out a new recipe. Having David cook for them was a perfect arrangement for Natalie, who claimed she couldn't even boil water without burning it.

Natalie had a child from a previous relationship, who lived with his father. Sadly, because of her hours at the restaurant, she rarely saw her son. The father, however, was a school teacher and was in a much better position to take care of him, so Natalie had agreed early on to let their son stay with his father.

David had never officially proposed, but they both knew that someday they would get married. They were even talking about having the wedding in the spring, with a few close family and friends. Nothing big, but David was looking forward to putting together a backyard barbecue for the celebration.

•   •   •   •   •

It was Friday morning. Natalie woke up and stretched, her arms reaching over her head. She looked to her left to see a lump under the sheets. She poked the lump and got a groan in response. She laughed and poked the lump again.

"Come on, sleepy head. It's time to get up," she said.

"Ugh. Are you serious?" David responded.

"Yup. We have to get ready and meet my mother for lunch. Remember?"

"Yeah, I guess. Why don't you get in the shower first, and that will give me a couple extra minutes to sleep," he suggested.

"Okay," she said, "but you'd better be ready to jump in the shower when I'm done."

"I will be," he promised, pulling the sheets over his head.

•   •   •   •   •

An hour later, David was driving on I-270, faster than Natalie liked. "C'mon, David. Slow down a bit, will you?"

"I will just as soon as I pass the little old lady in the twenty-foot-long Buick. She's as slow as molasses in January." Once he had safely maneuvered into the driving lane, he slowed down. "I swear, once a person is within sight of a hundred years old, they need to give up their license and start using Uber."

Natalie chuckled at his suggestion. "Well, we've got plenty of time before we meet Mom at the diner, so you don't need to feel rushed."

"What's the name of this diner again?" asked David.

"It's called the Silver Dollar Diner. She's been going there for years. She likes it because it's close to her house and it's not that expensive. Now that she's retired, she has to watch the cash flow."

"Do you think she's going to push us into setting the date?" David asked.

"Probably. When I spoke to her yesterday, she was hinting that she wants lots of grandkids."

"Seriously?" David gave Natalie a quick glance and an eye roll. "Good Lord. Is it too late for me to cancel this lunch? I think I have something to do back home."

Natalie laughed and gently punched his leg. "You do not. Besides, if she starts in on that kind of stuff, I'll cut her off and change the subject."

"Okay. I guess that'll work." David reached for Natalie's hand and gave her a squeeze.

·　　·　　·　　·　　·

True to her word, when Natalie's mom hinted that they should set a date for the wedding, Natalie changed the subject. It was an otherwise enjoyable luncheon, but before long, it was time to head home and get ready for work.

David and Natalie usually worked the evening shift and always together. Their boss, Michael Schumacher, set up the work schedules so that they could work the same shifts. Michael knew about their relationship, and couldn't be happier for them.

The evening at Rosalee's Restaurant was busy, as most Fridays were. When the last customers left, Michael locked the door behind them. As part of their usual routine at the end of the night, Natalie wiped down the dining room tables while David and Keshawn Walker, the other cook, cleaned up the kitchen. Michael emptied the cash registers and secured the cash in the safe in the manager's office.

Michael took one last look around the restaurant, satisfied that the place was neat and orderly, ready for the next day's business. They made it a practice to walk out together for safety's sake, so all four of them met in the storage room of the restaurant, near the back door.

They had no way of knowing that from that moment on, their lives would forever be changed.

Keshawn pushed on the crash bar that would open the door. Suddenly and without warning, a man barged through the door and flew into the restaurant, yelling and waving a gun in the air. He screamed at them to get on the floor. Startled, all four employees got down on their knees, and pressed their bodies to the floor.

CHAPTER SEVEN

Dusty, Maria, and Jorge were watching television in the living room. Maria and Jorge were sitting together on the couch, which also doubled as Dusty's bed. Dusty was sitting in a recliner.

He was nervously tapping his feet on the floor as if he was listening to a tune that only he could hear.

"What's your problem, dude?" asked Jorge, who was getting annoyed at Dusty's fidgeting.

"Nothing. Why, what's your problem?" Dusty answered with an attitude.

"Relax, man. You're bouncing around like your feet are on fire." Jorge hadn't taken offense at Dusty's comment.

"Yeah, well, I gotta go somewhere tonight and I'm waiting for my ride."

"What's up? You got a hot date or something?" Maria asked with a smile and a wink in Dusty's direction.

"No, just going out to catch a couple of beers with Shit Storm."

Maria rolled her eyes. She didn't like this guy Dusty referred to as Shit Storm and had told Dusty as much several times. "When are you going to ditch that guy? He's bad news." She knew McCracken was the person who got Dusty to fall off the wagon after he got out of prison, and she'd never forgiven him for it.

"Beggars can't be choosers, you know? It's not like I've got people falling at my feet wanting to hang out with me, like I'm the King of England or something." Dusty lifted himself out of the chair with a huff and left the room. Maria and Jorge eyed each other with raised eyebrows and turned to watch Dusty run up the stairs.

Dusty had been watching for McCracken from the bathroom window. When he finally saw headlights and watched the vehicle pull up to the curb, Dusty ran down the stairs and out the door, leaving Jorge and Maria to stare at the front door with curiosity.

Dusty opened the passenger door, and with one foot raised to step into the car, he stopped, his foot frozen in midair.

"What the hell?" he said. He focused his eyes on the back seat of the car.

"My old lady dropped Emma off a couple hours ago. Don't worry about it. She'll fall asleep in a little bit. She always does when she's in the car."

"Look, man. That wasn't part of the deal. I didn't want you to bring anyone else along." Dusty stared at the four-year-old who was watching a video on a child's iPad.

"What do you care? You're only going to be a few minutes, right? You go in, you make your deal, and I drive you home again. What's the problem?"

Dusty piled into the front seat with a scowl on his face. "Yeah, I guess it's alright." He realized he didn't have much of a choice at this point. "Let's go." He slammed the door shut, harder than he needed to, but the child's presence irritated him.

·   ·   ·   ·   ·

It was almost 1:00 AM on the dot when Dusty and McCracken pulled into the parking lot at Rosalee's Restaurant.

"No, man. Don't park here," Dusty said.

"What the hell are you talking about? I thought you wanted to go to Rosalee's?" McCracken raised his hands, palm up, in a sign of frustration. "You're acting crazy tonight, Dusty."

"Yeah, I know, but I don't want anyone to see the car. Park at the place next door, on the other side of those bushes." Dusty pointed to the long line of shrubbery that separated the two businesses.

"C'mon, man. This is ridiculous. What are you doing in there?" His friend was losing patience with Dusty.

"None of your business. Look, do you want your $100 or not?"

"Fine, man. Whatever." McCracken pulled into the roadway and made a quick left turn into the parking lot next door. "Hurry it up, though. I'm not waiting forever for your dumb ass."

Without a word, Dusty climbed out of the car and pulled at the back of his sweatshirt, making sure it covered the gun secreted in his waistband. Although a security light came on in front of the building, the parking lot on the passenger side of the car was too dark for McCracken to see what Dusty was doing.

McCracken looked at his daughter in the back seat. She had fallen asleep, the iPad still in her hand with the video playing.

As Dusty walked through a gap in the bushes and out of sight, he pulled a pair of clear, plastic gloves, similar to what they used in the restaurant, out of his pocket and put them on.

Twelve minutes later, Dusty came running straight through the bushes, swiping at the branches that tore at his sweatshirt. He flung the car door open, scaring McCracken, who had begun to doze off. His daughter woke up and started crying at the sudden noise. She dropped the iPad onto the car floor.

"Let's get the hell out of here! C'mon, man! Go! Go! Go!" Dusty screamed.

"Holy shit! What's going on?" McCracken turned the key in the ignition and pulled onto the roadway.

"I got two bodies on me." Dusty yelled over the child who was crying in the back seat.

"You got what? Are you saying you just killed two people?" McCracken's head spun between watching the road and looking at Dusty.

"Just drive! I gotta get outta here! I robbed the place and then I shot two people." Dusty had a wild, crazed look in his eye, one corner of his mouth turned up in a lopsided grin.

"Oh my God! What in the hell did you do that for? I can't believe you did that!" McCracken ran one hand through his hair, the other still on the steering wheel. "I gotta slow down before we draw attention to ourselves."

"Just keep driving. Head back to my house. It's cool. I had a mask on, so no one could identify me." Dusty still had the gun in his hand. He leaned forward so he could tuck it into the back of his waistband.

McCracken watched as his passenger hid the gun. "I thought you were going to buy drugs, man. You didn't tell me you were going to rob anyone. What did you have to shoot them for?"

Dusty had no answer. He just sat in the front seat, staring out the windshield. "Wait, a second. Slow down a bit. I want to throw the mask and my sweatshirt out the window." He pulled the mask and gloves from the front pocket of the sweatshirt.

"I can't believe this. You are an asshole, Dusty." McCracken slowed the car to a crawl and pulled to the shoulder of the highway. As he continued to drive at a slow pace on the shoulder, Dusty rolled down the window and threw out the mask and gloves. Then he wiggled out of the sweatshirt and threw that as far into the weeds as he could throw it.

Emma had stopped crying but was now wide-awake and sniffling. McCracken reached onto the floor of the back seat, found the iPad and gave it back to his daughter.

"I don't know how much I got, but I got some cash. I made the manager open the safe before I shot him." Dusty still had a crazed look about him.

"I can't freaking believe you did that. Are you out of your mind?" He looked at Dusty as if he expected an answer. "Look, Dusty, if you get caught, you'd better not get me involved. I had no idea you were going to kill people tonight. I thought you were buying drugs. What the hell?!" McCracken punched the steering wheel.

"Don't worry. That's why I had you park on the side. No one could see your car past those bushes. It's cool. You're not going to get involved."

McCracken shook his head, unable to comprehend what had just happened. They exchanged very few words as they drove the half-hour to where Dusty had been staying. McCracken was breathing heavily through his nose, his face contorted in anger. Dusty continued to look out the windshield with a look of satisfaction showing on his face. Little Emma had fallen back to sleep in the car seat.

McCracken pulled up in front of the house. Dusty reached for the handle on the car door, but turned to McCracken and said, "thanks, man. I appreciate it."

McCracken wouldn't even look at him. He kept his eyes straight ahead, without acknowledging Dusty's thank you.

"Yeah, well, I'll give you a call in the next day or two and give you your money." Dusty stepped out of the car, barely able to shut the door before McCracken sped away from the curb, squealing the tires.

By the time Dusty had gotten home, Jorge and Maria were already in bed. Dusty sat on the couch and separated the cash he had taken from Rosalee's into piles, just as he had done after he robbed the mom-and-pop store.

He counted the money three times. He held $536 in his shaking hands. After paying Amy and Vince, it would leave him with $36.

Dusty stared at the money and shook his head in disbelief. He had thought for sure there would be a lot more money in the safe. He figured the total take would be in the thousands, not the hundreds. All the trouble he'd gone through to formulate a plan, get a ride and a gun, not to mention killing two people, and all he had to show for it was thirty-six lousy freaking dollars. He couldn't believe it. What a freaking waste of time.

CHAPTER EIGHT

Sergeant Steve "Mac" MacIntosh was sound asleep in bed, with the images of a dream playing in his mind. As he traveled through the dream, he could see his ex-wife, Alayna, and his son, Austin, standing together on the top-most deck of a large cruise ship. Alayna lifted her chin, closed her eyes, and let the wind whip her auburn hair off her shoulders. Thirteen-year-old Austin, with a large grin, stretched his arms as wide as they would go, his hands cupped to catch the wind.

Mac was watching the scene play out as if he were a seagull flying high over their heads. Alayna and Austin stood at the bow of the ship, seemingly mesmerized by the ocean breeze as the ship cut through the water like a knife through butter.

The sound of the waves splashing on the hull was deafening, but in the dream, all Mac could hear was the ship's horn blasting the same two notes, waah, waaaaah, waah, waaaaah, over and over again, as if it were stuck.

With a reflexive jerk of his body, Mac woke up. The dream had ended, but the noise continued. Mac realized it was not a ship's horn that he had heard in the dream but the ringing of his cell phone. He reached for the phone just as the ringing stopped. He redirected his hand from reaching for the phone to rubbing his forehead.

"What the hell?" he muttered to himself. His heart was thumping in his chest from the adrenaline coursing through his veins. Mac swung his legs over and sat on the edge of the bed. He focused his still-blurry eyes on the alarm clock, the numbers illuminating the top of his nightstand. It was 1:20 Saturday morning.

The phone started ringing again, but this time, Mac was able to answer the call on the first ring.

"Yeah," he barked into the phone.

"Mac, this is Sergeant Marco DeLuca. We've got a bad one. We're going to need you to come in."

"What's going on?" He pinched the bridge of his nose in a feeble attempt to shake off the sleepiness and dull the adrenaline rush.

"We've got two people who have been shot to death at Rosalee's Restaurant on Boardwalk Place. The suspect got away," the sergeant explained.

"Oh, crap. Alright. Call in the rest of the CID team. Give me about twenty minutes and I'll be there." He hit the end call button.

Mac rubbed the stubble on his cheek as he took a deep breath. His heart was still racing after being pulled so suddenly out of a sound sleep. "What the hell," he said to himself again, as he reached for yesterday's pants draped across the foot of his bed.

·   ·   ·   ·   ·

Mac pulled into the parking lot of Rosalee's Restaurant, a nice family-style restaurant specializing in Italian fare that had been open for a good ten or fifteen years. Mac had eaten there a number of times over the years with Alayna and Austin. The building was constructed of large gray stones and windows that covered three of the four sides. A large green canopy covered the front walkway.

Mac took a quick look around to assess the scene as he got out of his car. The area was lit up like a carnival at night time with flashing blue, red, and white lights from the various emergency vehicles that were parked haphazardly around the building. The lights were bouncing off the restaurant's windows, creating a strobe effect that was almost blinding.

Police cars were parked at odd angles, abandoned where the first-arriving cops had left them as they sprinted from their vehicles and rushed into the restaurant. The ambulance crew was off to the side, standing by, even though they had already been told those who had been shot and killed would not need their services. The fire department was setting up the large spot lights that telescoped from the top of their trucks. Yellow caution tape had already been stretched around the entire restaurant and swayed gently in the light September breeze.

As Mac looked over the crime scene, he saw someone had propped open the back door to the restaurant with a stick shoved into the ground. One officer standing near the back was beckoning to him with a wave of his hand. Mac headed in that direction.

The officer met up with Mac and held out his hand. "Hey, Sarge. Good to see you."

Mac shook the officer's hand. "Hey, Marco. Good to see you too. I'd ask how you're doing on the night shift, but now is probably not a good time to ask." Mac looked solemnly over Marco's shoulder and lifted his chin towards the restaurant.

"Yeah, it's not good. We've got two bodies in the restaurant, but we've also got two witnesses that got out before they were injured. The witnesses are obviously pretty shaken up, but they've identified the suspect as a former co-worker."

"Any sign of the suspect?" Mac asked.

"No. He took off through the side door on the east side of the building, but nobody saw how he got away, whether he had a car or he took off on foot. We've got several patrol units scouting around in the area and I have a call into the Maryland State Police to see if they can send up their helicopter. I want to see if this guy might still be on foot somewhere nearby. I've asked for any available K9 units to respond as well."

"What's the response time for the K9 and the helicopter?" asked Mac.

"I called for both of them right before I called you. Luckily, the K9 unit was already on patrol close by, so they're sniffing around, as we speak." Marco looked at his watch. "I'd say it'll be about another five or ten minutes before the helicopter arrives."

"Good work. I'm going to head in and take a look at the scene. When the rest of my team shows up, have them come see me, would you?"

"Investigator Cooper is already here. He got here about two minutes before you did and went right into the restaurant." Marco hooked his thumb over his shoulder, towards the building.

"Okay. Thanks for the info." Mac hesitated for a moment and drew a deep cleansing breath before heading into the restaurant to join his partner.

Mac had been a cop for the last seventeen of his thirty-nine years and had been involved in literally thousands of police calls, but a homicide was always one of the worst. He shook his head as he regarded the senseless loss of life. That single, selfish act affected countless people. It never failed to amaze him how a person could feel the need, or think they had the right to take another person's life. What possible reason could they have for killing someone? Who knows what they'll find was the reason for tonight's killings?

As Mac approached the open back door, he noticed there was no doorknob on the outside of the door, although there was a crash bar on the inside. That told him that if entry was made through that back door, someone would have had to let the killer in.

An evidence technician was swirling black powder onto the door frame with a brush. With luck, the technician would be able to pick up fingerprints that belonged to the suspect. Mac bobbed his head to acknowledge the technician and carefully squeezed through the door, making sure he didn't disturb anything.

As Mac looked around, he could see that the area just inside the door appeared to be a small storage room. If it had been in a home, he would think of it as a mudroom. A body lay on the floor near the door, curled into the fetal position. Blood pooled underneath the victim's head.

He carefully walked towards the body. It appeared the victim, a male, had been shot at close range in the head.

Mac's partner, Investigator James "Coop" Cooper, stood a few feet away, in a short hallway that led towards the front of the restaurant. "Hey, Sarge. We've got another body in here."

Mac followed him. Off to the right was the kitchen, but to the left was what looked to be a small and cluttered office. Coop stopped and simply pointed towards that area. There was no need for words.

As Mac turned, he could see the second victim's feet, just past the partially opened door of the office. He headed in that direction.

"Do we have identification on the victims yet?" Mac asked over his shoulder.

"Yes, we do," said Coop. "The witnesses ID'd them both, and we've confirmed it with the identification in their wallets." He looked at the notes he had written in a small notebook in his hand. "The guy in the office is Michael Schumacher, the restaurant manager. There's a safe in there that's open and looks like it's been rummaged through. The guy in the back area where you just came from is a cook. His name is David Hamlin. One of the witnesses, Natalie Petrenko, is a server here, and she's also Hamlin's girlfriend. She's pretty broken up, but she's agreed to let Officer Eve Swanson take her back to the police department for a statement. The other witness is another cook by the name of Keshawn Walker, and they took him back for a statement. Officer Brian Collins is talking to him."

"Okay. I'm going to have a look around." Mac said. "It sounds like the helicopter is flying around out there now. Hopefully, they'll find this guy hiding in the weeds nearby."

Mac took a small notebook and pen out of his shirt pocket and began to make notations. He documented the scene with a sketch of the rooms and the positions of the bodies. He took notes of the names of the victims and survivors. Walking slowly from one area to the next, Mac was careful not to upset anything that could potentially be evidence.

From the open safe, Mac thought it was probably a robbery gone bad, but for now, he would not rush to any conclusions. He would wait until he had an opportunity to speak with the witnesses and the other members of the Criminal Investigations Division.

CHAPTER NINE

It was now 3:30 AM. Mac and his team of investigators had been at the scene of the double homicide for about two hours. The sun wouldn't rise and most people wouldn't wake to start their day for another few hours yet.

A helicopter had hovered over the area searching for the suspect, with no luck. The road patrol officers that had scoured the area had come up empty as well. The suspect was gone.

Mac had asked that a couple officers go to the victims' homes and make the difficult notifications to the families that their loved ones had been killed. They would need to be told right away, before they heard it from someone else or worse, saw it on social media.

Mac and Coop had worked diligently, poring over the scene, inch by inch, to try to piece together what might have happened in the restaurant. The evidence showed that it was a robbery gone bad, but they would know more once they talked to the witnesses.

Two evidence technicians, known as ETs, had combed the restaurant and the parking lot to collect anything and everything that might be helpful in their investigation.

Inside the restaurant, the ETs took photographs of the grisly scene before the coroner removed the bodies. They meticulously measured the rooms in the back of the restaurant and plotted where each piece of evidence had been recovered. They collected fingerprints, spent bullet casings and a single five-dollar bill that lay on the floor between the safe and Schumacher's body. The money had blood on it. The blood was probably Schumacher's, but they would have it analyzed just in case it was the suspect's blood. Perhaps he'd been wounded at some point.

There was a scrap piece of paper on the floor that had a partial shoe print on it, so they kept that as well. Maybe the paper had been stepped on by the suspect. It had happened before that a police agency had solved a crime by matching a footprint to a suspect's shoe.

Outside, on the grassy side of the building, the ETs found two beer bottles and carefully placed them in plastic evidence bags. They would test them later to see if there was any DNA or fingerprints on them. Although they could have been dropped by someone not related to the homicides, it's possible the suspect had left them behind.

With his investigative duties at the scene completed, Mac headed back to the police department in his vehicle. Coop had already gone back to the PD about a half hour before.

By now, the witnesses would have already given their statements to other police officers, but Mac had called the station as he was leaving the restaurant and asked if the witnesses would wait a few more minutes before going home. He wanted to talk to them as well.

It had been a long night for the witnesses, but they were willing to stick around for a bit longer, eager to tell their stories in the hopes of catching their co-workers' killer.

Mac walked into the police station and headed to the office. Coop was already sitting at his desk, so they took a few moments to talk. It was the first chance they'd had to compare notes.

"We'll know more when we talk to the witnesses," Mac was saying to Coop, "but it looks like the suspect was after money. I want to know how he got into the restaurant, though. Did they let him in after-hours since they knew him, or was he already there, maybe hanging out in the bar area before closing time? That might tell us if he was working alone, or if he had an accomplice."

"I've started working on the suspect's possible whereabouts," added Coop. "The witnesses didn't think he lived here in Gaithersburg. They thought he lived out of town somewhere, but they weren't positive. I've got a call in to the general manager to see if she can get us this guy's home address. She wasn't too happy getting a call in the middle of the night until I explained what had happened. She's pretty upset and said she'd help with anything we need. I'm hoping she can get us the video from the security camera, too. She said she can remote into the restaurant's computer from her laptop at home to check the personnel records and the video. She'll stop by here when she has everything."

"Yeah, that's perfect," Mac said. "I'm going to fix a quick cup of coffee while I run Sampson through the computer system to see if he's been arrested before. It would be great if we can get a mugshot of him. Then we can show a photo array to the witnesses and see if they can positively identify him. If you want to talk to one witness, I'll talk to the other. I'm sure they want to get home by now and if we split up, they'll be on their way that much sooner."

"Sounds like a plan, boss." Coop sat at his computer and opened the state criminal history program. It did not surprise him when Dusty Sampson's name appeared. He quickly made a photo array, combining Dusty's photo with the photos of five similar-looking men. This is known as a six-pack because of the total of six photos, three in the top row and three in the bottom.

Coop printed out two copies of the photo array, gave one to Mac and kept the other.

Investigator Cooper offered to interview the cook, Keshawn Walker, while Mac talked to the other witness, Natalie Petrenko. As he entered the interview room, Coop could see the mix of emotions on Walker's face. There was no doubt the man was physically and emotionally exhausted after the horrible night, but there was also shock and sadness in his eyes. Coop introduced himself and shook Walker's hand.

"You've been through a horrible ordeal," began Coop, "so we'll try to make this as quick as possible so you can be on your way. I'm sure you're anxious to get home."

"Yeah, thanks, man. It's been one hell of a night. I still can't believe it." Walker rubbed his eyes with the heel of his hands. "Nobody is telling me anything. What happened to Schumacher and Hamlin? Are they okay?"

"No, I'm sorry. They both died at the scene," Coop said softly.

"Oh, my God. I had a feeling that's why nobody wanted to tell me what was going on." Walker put his head in his hands. "That's not right. They were good people. Both of them. They didn't deserve that."

"You told the officers earlier that you knew the suspect. Is that right?" Coop asked.

"Yeah, his name is Dusty Sampson. He worked at Rosalee's as a dishwasher until about three months ago. He was a nice-enough guy, but he kept missing a lot of work, so they had to let him go. I think he was into drugs."

"How do you know it was Dusty who came into the restaurant tonight?"

"Well," explained Walker, "I couldn't see his face because he was wearing a mask, like a bandana wrapped around his nose and mouth, but I could tell it was him by his voice. He's got a raspy voice, but it's kind of high-pitched for a man."

Coop pushed the photo array of Dusty Sampson across the table. "Do you see Dusty Sampson on this photo array?"

"Yeah, that's him," Keshawn said without hesitation, as he pointed to the center photo in the bottom row. Keshawn had positively identified Dusty Sampson's photo.

Coop handed Keshawn a pen. "Would you circle the photo and then put your initials next to the one you've pointed out as Sampson's?"

Keshawn circled Dusty's photo several times before putting his initials near the photo.

"Can you tell me what happened tonight?" asked Coop.

Walker took a deep breath. "We were just leaving for the night. We always leave as a group to make sure everyone gets out safely." He stopped when he realized what he had just said. "I guess it didn't work this time, did it?"

Coop gave his witness a moment to compose himself and then pressed him to continue. "Who was in the group that was walking out with you?"

"It was me, Hamlin, Schumacher and Petrenko. Hamlin and Petrenko are going out together. Anyway, I was the one that opened the door. I couldn't tell he was on the other side because there's no window in the door and there's no doorknob on the outside either. Nobody uses that door to get in because you can't get in unless someone on the inside opens the door for them. It scared the shit out of me because I didn't expect anyone to be there. He just pushed his way in as soon as I opened the door."

"What happened next?" asked Coop.

"Sampson was waving a gun around. He was mostly pointing it at Schumacher, but he'd look at the rest of us and point it at us, too. Hamlin and Schumacher put their hands up in the air. I don't know if Petrenko did, but I know I did. Then Sampson told us all to lie on the floor, so we did."

"Do you know what kind of gun it was?"

"Not really. It looked like the kind that you've got." Keshawn pointed to Coop's hip, where his 9mm police-issued gun was holstered.

"The whole time, Sampson was yelling that he wanted money. He told Schumacher to get up and go into the office to open the safe, that he knew there would be money in there.

Schumacher kept telling Sampson not to shoot. I think he was trying to keep Sampson calm because he was trying to talk like he was calm. He said he would get him the money and to just relax.

"So, Schumacher got up and went into the office, but the rest of us stayed on the floor. I think we were all too shocked and too scared to move. Sampson stayed in the hallway so he could keep an eye on

Schumacher and us at the same time. I don't think I'll ever forget the look in his eyes. His eyes were wild. It was like he was a crazy man. He just kept yelling at us and waving that damn gun around."

"What was he saying?" asked Coop.

"He was telling Schumacher to hurry up and get him the effing money and he kept telling us not to move.

"Then I heard Schumacher tell Sampson that he had the safe open, so Sampson ran into the office. Schumacher kept telling him he didn't have to do this. Schumacher kept telling Sampson that if he would just leave, he wouldn't even call the police. Then I heard Sampson tell Schumacher, 'you know it's over, right?'" Then I heard a gunshot and Sampson was running towards us. He still had the gun in one hand, but he had a fistful of money in the other hand. The rest of us were still on the floor, so he stood over Hamlin and shot him. For no reason at all, he just shot him in the head.

"Then he pointed the gun at Petrenko, and she was begging him not to shoot her. She kept telling him she's got a kid and he needs his mom. He kept pulling the trigger anyway, but it didn't fire. I think the gun jammed because he started knocking on it with his hand, like he was trying to get it unjammed. That's when Natalie jumped up and ran towards the office where Schumacher was and I got up and ran out the side door. Once I was outside, I ran like hell to the other side of the restaurant and hid in the building's shadow next door until the cops came."

"Did you see Sampson leave?" Coop asked.

"No, but I heard him running behind me, out the side door. I went in one direction and I think he went in the other, but I didn't see exactly where he was going, though. Like I said, I took off running, and I didn't look back. I was afraid if I slowed down, he'd shoot me, too."

"Okay, Mr. Walker," Coop said as he stood up, "if we have any more questions, I'll let you know, but we're all set for now. Did you leave your car at Rosalee's? I can have one of our officers drive you back there if you would like."

"Yeah, that would be great. I'm in no hurry to see the place, but I need to get my car." Walker spoke very softly.

"Okay. If you can wait here for just a minute, I'll get someone to take you back." Coop reached over the table to shake Walker's hand. Walker looked like he would need every ounce of energy to lift himself off the chair. The shock and stress of the night's events were obviously weighing on him.

After making the arrangements for the ride, Coop went into the Criminal Investigations Division, or CID, office he shared with the other investigators. As soon as Coop sat down at his desk, he began poring over the notes he had taken while he had been talking with Walker. A few minutes later, Mac came in. His interview with Petrenko also finished.

"I've got a good lead from Natalie Petrenko as to where the suspect might live," began Mac. "She said she'd given him a ride home from work a couple of times. She didn't know the address, but she could show us if we drove her there, so I've got Officer Eve Swanson driving her to that location. Petrenko confirmed that the address was local, not out of town. She also positively identified Sampson's photo on the six-pack."

"My guy positively identified him as well. Looks like we have a bingo," said Coop.

Within a few more minutes, the rest of the CID team returned from the scene of the crime and settled at their desks in the office.

Mac looked around the office at the men working on their computers. He had good people on his team and he knew they would do the best that they could do to find the suspect.

Investigator James Cooper, otherwise known as Coop, had been with CID almost as long as Mac. He was thirty-five years old and single, which is just the way he liked it. There was, however, no shortage of women to date in his little black book, a fact that he liked to point out in jest as often as he could. Coop was full of energy and brought humor to the team, although he also had a serious side that proved to be invaluable to the department. He had a knack for getting suspects to talk when no one else could.

Investigator Brandon Powers was the oldest member of the group. At forty-six years old, he was also an evidence technician, with a strength in photography. He was especially skilled at taking evidence photos, and by adjusting the lighting and camera exposure, he was able to capture photos that were fool-proof pieces of evidence that would stand up in court.

Investigator Patrick O'Malley was the youngest, at thirty-two years old. He had come from a law enforcement family, following in the steps of his father and grandfather. He was also an evidence technician, but his specialty was in forensic evidence. O'Malley could collect DNA and fingerprints from even the most difficult surfaces.

Mac himself had been an investigator for the last seven years. When the previous CID sergeant had retired five years ago, it was a no-brainer that Mac should replace him as the next sergeant. He was even-tempered, which came in handy when dealing with difficult people - criminals, suspects, victims or witnesses. Most importantly, he earned the respect of his fellow officers because he could think quickly and efficiently when the situation called for it.

Mac came out of his reverie with a subtle shake of his head. He needed to focus on the work, since time was of the essence. They would compare notes and bounce ideas off of each other to come up with a game plan, while they waited for confirmation of the address from Eve Swanson. A murderer was on the loose, and they needed to find him before someone else got hurt.

CHAPTER TEN

Mac and his team of investigators gathered around the small, round table in the CID office at the police department with their notebooks in front of them.

Coop had just finished talking to the witness, Keshawn Walker, while Mac had spoken to the other witness, Natalie Petrenko. Now, as a team, they would exchange information and figure out their next steps.

Coop was the first to share what he'd learned with his co-workers that Walker had identified a former employee, Dusty Sampson, as the killer. Walker had said that Sampson had forced his way into the restaurant and demanded money. He'd then shot two employees in cold blood and attempted to shoot Petrenko. The only reason Petrenko and Walker survived the attack was because Sampson's gun had jammed.

"My witness, Natalie Petrenko, said the same thing," explained Mac, "and she also identified Sampson as the killer. She said he was wearing a mask, but she could see a tattoo of a troll on this guy's wrist when his sleeve rose a bit. She said Sampson has the same tattoo, and she recognized it immediately."

"Wait a minute. You said he has a troll tattoo?" asked Investigator Patrick O'Malley. "You mean, like the toy with the bushy hair that stands straight up from its head? That kind of troll?"

"Yep. Sounds weird to me, but that's what she said," said Mac. "She'd given Sampson a ride home after work a couple of times. She didn't know the exact address, but she knows right where it is, and she said it's local. She's riding with Eve Swanson now, showing her where the house is. They should be back shortly.

"Coop found out from a background check that this guy Sampson has a criminal history, so he was able to get his mugshot, but we need to get more information. We didn't take the time to go over his history when Coop made the photo arrays, so I want to check further into his criminal history, his addresses, see if he has a vehicle and get a list of his accomplices. I'd like to see if the background check also shows a troll tattoo on his wrist. Patrick, can you follow up on all that?"

O'Malley nodded his head. "Sure thing, boss."

When Coop had been looking for the mugshot, he had checked in the Montgomery County criminal history database. Besides the photo, it also lists pedigree information, such as date of birth, any known addresses, height, weight and any tattoos, birthmarks or scars the individual was known to have.

Now, Patrick would check Sampson's criminal history in the National Crime Information Center, commonly known as NCIC. It would list any crimes an individual, or in this case, Sampson, might have committed anywhere in the country. Within minutes, by running him through the NCIC, Patrick found that the only crimes listed for Sampson had been committed in Maryland.

"Has the general manager come in yet with the security video and the suspect's personnel file?" Mac asked.

Investigator Brandon Powers slid a few pages of paper across the table towards Mac. "She dropped this off while you were in the interview with Petrenko. I skimmed through it and found his address. He's listed a Rockville address on his employment paperwork, although that doesn't seem to match what Natalie Petrenko is saying. The manager also gave us the security video on a thumb drive, but I haven't had a chance to look at it yet. I'll look at that as soon as we're done here."

"Okay. Brandon, why don't you check out the video now and see what you can find out. We need to know where he went after he left the restaurant. Was he on foot or did he get into a car, and if he got into a car, was he alone or did he have an accomplice? O'Malley, while you're digging in the computer on this guy, I'd like you to check out his associates. See if he has a girlfriend or a parent he might run to. Then see if you can do a background check on them. I'm especially interested in their addresses.

"Coop, I'd like you to see if he has any social media pages. Almost everybody has at least a Facebook page nowadays. I want to see if he was stupid enough to post something about the robbery. I'm going to start typing up an arrest warrant and a search warrant for his residence and getting that ready for the judge to sign. If Natalie Petrenko can get us a good address for the suspect, I'll fill in that part on the search warrant when they get back, but I'll get it started at least. I don't want to waste time because we need to find this guy before he kills anyone else."

"Sounds good, boss," said Coop. All four men turned to their computers. For the next several minutes, the only noise that could be heard was the tap, tap, tapping of their keyboards as they got right to work.

It wasn't long before Ofc. Eve Swanson and Natalie Petrenko were back with an address for Dusty Sampson. O'Malley checked the address against those listed for Dusty in the NCIC. They were in luck - the address was Dusty's mother's house, located right there in Gaithersburg.

Mac took Eve aside and asked her to drive Natalie back to the restaurant to retrieve her car.

"Actually, Sarge, I'm way ahead of you," Eve admitted. "I've already asked her if I could, but she said she was worn out and she couldn't face going back to the restaurant. She said she would worry about the car later, so I'm going to take her home instead."

"Thanks, Eve. I'm sure she appreciates that," Mac said with a smile.

· · · · ·

Now that they had an address for their suspect, Mac could complete the search warrant. The sun was just beginning to peek over the horizon and even though it was 6:45 in the morning, Mac called Judge Evelyn Johannsen at home to ask if she would sign the warrants. An early riser, she was already up and was just heading in to work herself. She said she would meet Mac at her office in half an hour.

Early morning had always been Mac's favorite time of day. He enjoyed taking walks through the neighborhood whenever he had the time. Before the divorce, he and Alayna used to enjoy going for early morning walks as a way to spend quiet time together before the daily hustle and bustle of life began.

Mac enjoyed the beautiful reds, yellows and oranges that colored the sky of the Maryland sunrise. He found the soft chirps of the birds as they were waking up to be a soothing, meditative way to start his day.

Today, however, he didn't notice the sky or the birds. His focus was entirely on the homicide; getting justice for the victims by finding the suspect, Dusty Sampson. Rather than going for his usual morning walk, he drove as quickly as he could to Judge Johannsen's office with the warrants beside him on the car seat.

The Judge was already at the office by the time Mac got there. She had heard about the double homicide from the local news, but asked Mac to fill her in on the details.

He gave her the abridged version. "We believe it was a robbery gone bad," Mac explained. "According to the witnesses, the suspect barged through the back door at closing time, brandishing a gun. He held the staff at gunpoint and demanded that the manager open the safe. The suspect grabbed the cash from the safe, but then he shot the manager and a cook in cold blood. He then attempted to shoot a server, but lucky for her, the gun apparently jammed. The server and the other witness both took off at that point. Both witnesses identified the suspect as a former co-worker named Dusty Sampson. They both said the suspect had a unique voice, and the server also said she saw a troll tattoo on his wrist."

The Judge listened intently as Mac relayed the information. He handed her the witness's written statements and the mug shots. She carefully looked them over, and without another word, signed the warrants.

·　·　·　·　·

An hour later, with the warrants in hand, Mac and the rest of the CID investigators met with the Warrant Entry Team, or WET team, as they were called. This specialized team spent hours and hours each year in training so that they could safely enter a building, complete a search, and find their suspect in a matter of minutes.

Considering that Dusty was known to have a gun, Mac asked a few additional officers to go with them for manpower. Together, the officers, the CID investigators and the WET team mapped out a plan to converge on the house and hopefully take Sampson into custody.

Mac gave everyone a specific duty. The WET team would split up, with most of them making entry into the home. The others would stay outside in case Dusty or anyone else tried to escape. Those officers that entered the home would then search the various rooms. The rest of the officers and CID would follow right on their heels and would take Dusty into custody if he was there. Mac would hold on to the warrants until they were needed.

CID drove in their vehicles to the address their witness provided, while the WET team and extra officers rode in the specialized mobile command vehicle. As soon as the over-sized van slowed to a near stop, the WET team members flew out of the back of the van and within seconds, surrounded the home. Once everyone was in place, an officer pounded on the door with his fist and yelled, "Police! Open up!"

Moments later, just seconds before an officer was preparing to hit the door with a large battering ram, the door was opened by a wide-eyed woman wearing a short fleece bathrobe and holding a lit cigarette in her hand. The WET team barged through the door and into her home, forcing her to step aside or get run over by the heavily armed men.

"What the hell is going on?" she yelled, but no one stopped to answer her. "What are you people doing?"

Mac and Coop entered the home and found the woman standing beside the door, her hand still on the doorknob.

"What the hell is going on? What are you doing in my house?" She looked at Mac and Coop, her eyes going back and forth between them.

"Ma'am, we're looking for Dusty Sampson. Do you know him? Do you know where he is?" Mac asked.

"He's my son." Mac handed her the search warrant as she spoke.

She looked at the paper in her hand. Her voice dropped to a whisper. "What do you want him for?"

"We'd like to talk to him. Do you know where he is?"

"No, I don't." She tipped her head and looked at Mac out of the corner of her eyes, as if she was afraid to ask, "What's he done?"

"Are you sure you don't know where he is?" Mac pressed.

Dolores walked towards the coffee table in the living room, tossed the warrant on the table, and stubbed out her cigarette in the ashtray. She grabbed another cigarette from a pack on the table and lit it with a lighter. She drew in a deep puff of the cigarette. "He doesn't live here anymore. I threw his ass out for the last time a few months ago. Last I knew, he was living with a friend of his in Rockville, but I don't know where. He stops in once in a while, but usually it's only if he needs money. Are you going to tell me what he's done or not?"

"We just need to talk to him." Mac repeated. The house stunk of stale cigarette smoke and a light haze hung in the air. He was trying hard not to breathe in the smoke. "Do you have his cell phone number?"

"He buys those burner phones, and he's always getting new numbers, so I can't keep them straight. Most of the time they get shut off anyway, because he can't pay for the service. If I need to talk to him, I usually use Facebook Messenger."

Mac and Coop looked at each other. "What's the name he uses on his Facebook account?" Coop asked. He took a pad and pen out of his jacket pocket.

"It's 'Troll Boy,' I think. Something like that." Dolores waved her hand to the side. The ashes fell from the tip of her cigarette onto the rug. She didn't seem to notice.

"Ma'am, do you have a computer?" Mac asked.

"Sure, doesn't everybody nowadays?"

"We'd like to see it. Would you show me where it is, please?"

"It's on the kitchen counter. I was just checking out the coupons for the Giant grocery store when you came barging in." Dolores raised her chin, as if showing that she didn't appreciate his presence in her home.

"Ma'am, we'll need to take it as part of our investigation. You'll be able to get it back though, just as soon as we're done with it."

"Whatever. I don't care. The thing is a cheap piece of shit, anyway."

Coop grabbed the laptop and power cord and placed them in a plastic bag. When they got back to the station, they would go through the computer's history and try to get more information on Dusty's whereabouts.

The WET team leader stood in front of Mac and gave the signal that the home was all clear. Dusty was not there.

Mac thanked Dolores for her time as the WET team and CID members filed out of the home. Dolores stood in the living room, frozen in place. "What did he do?" she asked, more emphatically.

Her eyes remained glued to the front door as Mac pulled it closed behind him. He still hadn't answered her.

"Dusty... what have you done now?" she whispered to herself.

Chapter Eleven

Dusty pushed the $500 intended for Amy and Vince to the side of the coffee table and looked at the remaining $36 he held in his hand. A twenty, a ten and six ones. He crumpled the bills in his fist, angry that $36 was all he would show for his efforts. There's no way he could settle for that.

He couldn't believe he hadn't gotten enough money after robbing Rosalee's and killing two people to pay his bills and still leave enough to get him out of town.

Dusty paced in circles in the living room. He didn't have any choice now. He was definitely going to have to rob another place. Vince wanted the gun back Sunday morning, so at least he had time before he had to return the weapon.

The bigger problem was going to be getting a ride. McCracken was pretty pissed off at him, so there's no way he would give Dusty another ride. Plus, he still owed McCracken $100 for the ride to Rosalee's, and he didn't even have enough money to pay that. *Maybe he could get an Uber,* he thought. *No, that's not cool. I'd have to pay them, too.*

Dusty struggled with a plan, one that would get him cash, but wouldn't cost him any additional money for things like a ride. The only thing he could think of was to rob a gas station. Some gas stations are also convenience stores, he reasoned, and they would probably have the cash he needed.

Since the options for transportation to the next job were extremely limited, Dusty decided he would have to find a place fairly close by so that he could walk there and back, preferably after sunset, when it would be too dark to be followed. With that in mind, he realized there weren't that many convenience stores in the area that would be close enough to walk to and would also be open later in the evening.

However, there was one place that came to mind. The Omega Shop was a gas station, a convenience store, and a car wash all rolled into one. It seemed to Dusty that there was always a line for the car wash and there seemed to be a steady line of people going in and out of the store.

Plus, it was only about a half-mile away. He had his answer. He would rob The Omega Shop the next night. *Actually,* thought Dusty, *that would be tonight. It's already Saturday.*

Dusty laid down on the couch and closed his eyes, a satisfied smile pulling at the corners of his mouth. He was asleep in a matter of minutes.

·　　·　　·　　·　　·

Dusty slept until noon, before finally waking up. Jorge and Maria were already gone, having left the house a couple of hours earlier.

Knowing he was alone in the house, Dusty took advantage of the opportunity and checked out the gun. He wanted to know why it had jammed. Unfortunately, Dusty knew nothing about taking guns apart or cleaning them, and he couldn't tell by simply looking at the gun why it had jammed. So he simply tossed it from one hand to the next and banged it against the palm of his hand. He shrugged his shoulders and stuffed it in the bottom of his backpack.

To keep busy, Dusty floated between watching Netflix on TV and checking his Facebook page for messages. Neither one held his interest, so the day dragged on.

He was trying hard not to think about the two people he had shot and killed the night before. When he thought about what happened, he got angry. He didn't really want to kill them, but he also didn't want to leave witnesses. If Schumacher had just handed over the cash like he'd asked, he wouldn't have had to shoot him. Dusty would have just taken the money and left. But Schumacher was trying to bullshit him by saying that he wouldn't even call the police, as long as Dusty forgot about the money and just left. Well, that wasn't going to happen. He needed the money. End of story.

Jorge and Maria returned to the house with a few of their friends about six o'clock. They ordered a couple of pizzas and Buffalo wings for dinner and invited Dusty to join them. He gave them $10 towards the dinner, which left him with $26. It reminded him of how little money he had. Dusty was feeling anxious, knowing that he would rob the convenience store in a couple more hours.

"What's going on, Dusty?" asked Jorge. "Are you alright? You've been real edgy lately."

"Yeah, I'm fine," Dusty lied. "I just have a lot on my mind, is all."

"You need to get yourself a girlfriend, to take your mind off everything," said Maria. "You haven't dated anyone since Destiny broke up with you six months ago."

"It's hard to get a girlfriend when I haven't got any money." Dusty got up, scraping the chair legs on the linoleum floor with a loud screeching noise. He went into the living room and laid on the couch.

With one hand over his head, Dusty stared at the ceiling. He was having second thoughts about robbing the store. But what choice did he have? Especially now that he'd killed two people, he needed the money to get the hell out of town.

Finally, a little after 8:00 PM, Dusty left the house and started walking on his way to The Omega Shop. He had the gun hidden in the back of his belt under the sweatshirt, and the red bandana wrapped around his neck. He'd tucked it into the collar of his sweatshirt so it would remain hidden until he pulled it out to cover his nose and mouth. The thought made him think of the old Western movies where the bad guy always wore a bandana over the lower half of his face.

Once he got to The Omega, Dusty hung out at the corner of the building, watching as people came and went. Just like he did before at the mom-and-pop grocery store, he wanted to make sure no other customers were in there. Finally, after waiting about twenty minutes, the last customer left. Dusty knew the store was empty, except for the store employee behind the counter. It was almost closing time, so the parade of customers had slowed down considerably.

Dusty pulled the bandana over his nose and the gun from his belt. He walked into the store and, after glancing around, he saw the cashier behind the counter, on the right-hand side of the store. Their eyes met.

The cashier, a young woman about eighteen or nineteen years old, screamed.

"Open the register! Open it now!" Dusty shouted at her as he pointed the gun at her head.

"Oh, my God! Don't shoot me!" she yelled back, raising her hands high above her.

"Give me the money. I want all of it!" Dusty continued to yell.

The young woman reached over and hit a button on the cash register. The drawer popped open. She stepped back, her butt hitting the shelves of cigarettes behind her, a couple of packs hitting the floor.

Dusty reached over the counter and grabbed the bills that were in the divided sections of the cash tray. "Lift it up. Lift that tray," Dusty yelled as he waved the gun, aiming anywhere from her head to her stomach.

Cautiously, she leaned over and pulled the plastic tray out of the register, letting it fall to the floor with a loud crash. Coins fell out of the tray and scattered across the floor, some rolling under the counter. She quickly stepped back, tightly butting up to the cigarette display again. Dusty grabbed the five or six $50 bills that had been hidden in the bottom of the drawer under the tray.

"Don't you dare call the police," Dusty warned. "I'll be waiting outside for the next ten minutes. If I see a cop car anywhere near here, I'll come back in and kill you." Dusty turned and ran out the door. Regardless of the threat he made to the cashier, he continued running and didn't stop until he got home.

If he had truly waited at The Omega like he had threatened to do, he would have seen a small army of police cars responding to the silent alarm that signaled a robbery in progress. The cashier had pushed the button under the counter as soon as her eyes met Dusty's.

By the time Dusty got home, Jorge and Maria had gone upstairs to their room. *Perfect!* he thought. *I can count the money and see how much I got without them knowing anything about what happened.*

Dusty laid the $50 bills in a pile on the coffee table, then the twenty's, ten's, five's and one's. It was easier for him to count it that way. Once it was all said and done, he had counted $1,582 in cash. *Holy shit,* Dusty thought. *I've never had so much money in my whole life!*

Dusty was happy, in a way he hadn't been in a long time. In order to celebrate his windfall, he headed around the corner to the liquor store. He bought himself a pint of Jameson's Irish whiskey, proudly putting the cash on the counter. As soon as he stepped onto the sidewalk, he popped open the bottle and took a long pull.

By the time he fell asleep on the couch that night, the bottle would be almost empty and Dusty would be very drunk.

Chapter Twelve

It was 6:00 PM Saturday, almost seventeen hours since the homicides. Mac and the team of investigators were over-tired, but the need to locate and arrest their suspect, along with a lot of coffee, kept them pushing forward.

Anita, the civilian clerk, walked into the CID office loaded down with a platter of sandwiches.

"Come and get it!"

Coop was the first one out of his chair. He grabbed Anita by the shoulders and gave her a quick peck on the cheek. "Anita, you're the best! We've had nothing to eat all day except for snacks from the vending machine."

Anita laughed, her cheeks turning red. "Well, I figured you'd probably be pretty hungry by now, and I knew you wouldn't take the time to order anything on your own. Hold on, I've got cold bottles of water and homemade chocolate chip cookies to bring in as well. I would have been here sooner, but I hadn't heard about the homicides until a little while ago. I was babysitting my grandkids at my son's house all morning."

The investigators each grabbed some food and headed to their desks. They would eat while they worked.

Having Dolores Sampson's laptop computer was a lucky break for the detectives. Brandon Powers lifted the cover and the computer sprang to life. It was not password protected, so Brandon was able to open up Dolores' Facebook page. He clicked on the Messenger button and found Troll Boy in the list of conversations. They had struck gold. A long list of messages between Dusty and his mother was displayed on the screen.

Brandon could then click on Dusty's profile from the Messenger tab. He had posted very few posts and even fewer photos on his home page. It seemed that he was more active on Messenger than anything else.

"Mac, I've got Dusty's profile page on Facebook," Brandon announced.

"Perfect. I can use that to get Dusty's IP address and find out where he lives. I've got a buddy in the FBI that can help," Mac said.

Mac knew that every computer and cell phone, when hooked up to the internet, had its own unique identifier known as an IP address. The IP address is a string of numbers that lets the internet provider know where to send such things as your email and data. It's similar to having a street address, so that the post office knows where to send your mail.

Based on the IP address, the FBI could tell where the computer was physically located. However, if he wanted any more information than that, Mac would have to get a warrant, but at least for now, he could get the home address. That would be a major step in finding the suspect.

Now that they had the profile information from Dusty's Facebook page, Mac called his buddy in the FBI. As he placed the call from his cell phone, he left the CID office, preferring to pace up and down the hall, too amped up to sit still at his desk.

"Hey, Rich. This is Steve MacIntosh."

"Hi, Mac. How are you?"

"Not bad. How are you doing? How's Elizabeth?"

"She's doing great. The cancer is in remission, so we're keeping our fingers crossed that it stays that way."

"That's great news, Rich. Tell her I send my love. Say, I'm calling to see if you can run a Facebook profile on a guy and find out where his computer is."

"Sure, I can do that. Do you have a warrant for this one?"

"No, but I don't need it this time because I'm making the request under exigent circumstances. We had a robbery with a double homicide last night. We've got the suspect's Facebook name, so I'm hoping you can get us the IP address. That should tell us where he's living."

"Holy crap. Double homicide, eh? Yeah, I can definitely get you that information." Rich said. "Give me just a second to open up the right program, and we'll be good to go." Mac could hear the keys clicking on the other end of the phone as Rich was typing.

Mac gave Rich the information that Dusty had adopted 'Troll Boy' as his Facebook name, and that he was living somewhere in the Gaithersburg/Rockville area. Within a few minutes, Rich was able to supply the physical address located in Rockville. He went one step further and tapped directly into Dusty's Facebook page. From there, he could check out all of Dusty's messages, not just the ones between Dusty and his mother. Rich was horrified by what he read.

"Your suspect, Dusty Sampson, has been messaging with some woman about getting a gun," Rich explained. "She goes by the name Amy Hoffmann on Facebook. From the messages, it looks like she arranged the whole thing between Dusty and some guy she calls Vince for Dusty to buy the gun. I haven't got Vince's full name."

"Oh, shit! That's huge!" said Mac.

"Wait until you hear the rest of it. Dusty wrote that he was planning to rob Rosalee's on Friday night, then another place on Saturday night. He said that he was going to lie low on Sunday, rob a bank first thing Monday morning and then head out of town right after that, with the cash he gets from the robberies."

"Did he mention what restaurant he was going to hit on Saturday night?" Mac asked.

"No, not by name. Just that he wanted to rob some places, and then get the hell out of Dodge."

"We need to catch this guy before he kills anyone else. From what he's saying in those messages, he'll be robbing another place tonight." Mac rubbed his forehead as an outward sign of the stress he was feeling.

Rich said that according to the dates on the messages - including one from the day before - it appeared Dusty had been staying at this particular home for a few months, which coincided with the information his mother had given Mac. Dolores said she'd thrown him out a few months before, and that seemed to be how long he'd been using that computer.

Rich continued to review the messages that Dusty, aka Troll Boy, had sent and received. He concentrated on the messages between Dusty and the woman known as Amy Hoffman about getting a gun. Five days before the homicides, Dusty had written to her, "I have to have protection in order to complete the job. This ain't a joke. We all want to get paid, right?"

"Listen, Mac," Rich said. "I'm going to send you copies of what I have for now from Dusty's messages. It's enough for you to get your warrant to search Dusty's house. If you can grab his computer in the search, you'll have it, anyway. If not, give me a call back and I'll get whatever you need."

"Thanks, Rich. I appreciate your help. I definitely owe you one."

"Yeah, yeah. Add it to the list," joked Rich.

． ． ． ． ．

Mac returned to the CID office and told the other investigators what Rich had found.

Now it was time to write up another search warrant, but this time, it would be for the house where the messages written by Dusty had originated from. They needed to get in the house as soon as humanly possible to see if Dusty was there. Once in the house, they would also look to see if they could find any evidence that linked Dusty to the homicides at Rosalee's Restaurant, especially his computer.

Mac asked Investigator Patrick O'Malley to draw up the search warrant. O'Malley was an excellent investigator, a quick thinker, and could type much faster than Mac, whose method was pecking at the keys, one finger at a time.

"While we're waiting for the judge to sign the warrant on the house," Mac said, "we need to find out if Dusty is staying there. It sounds like he is, but if he's planning another robbery for tonight, we don't have time to play games. We need to find him, like now. Brandon, I'd like you to go to that address and stake out the house. See if you can spot him going in or out. Don't stop him yet. I want the warrant in hand before we do that. Just find out if he's still at that house."

"You got it, Mac. I'm on my way." Brandon grabbed his bullet-proof vest and headed out the door.

Mac returned to his desk and, with a heavy sigh, picked up the phone. He needed to call his son. Mac was supposed to take Austin to the Baltimore Orioles game in an hour, but he obviously wouldn't be able to make it. He didn't like missing quality time with this son, but sometimes it couldn't be avoided.

Mac, his wife, and their son had been a close-knit family, and in a lot of ways, they still were. But Mac and Alayna had divorced a few years before when, as the wife of a cop, the demands of his job became too much for her.

In the beginning of his career, Mac had worked the road patrol, and he occasionally missed important family mile markers like birthdays, holidays, and school concerts because of his work hours. But as a road patrol cop, once he was off duty, he generally stayed off the clock, and rarely got called back into work.

However, when he became an investigator about seven years ago, there were many times when he got called back to work for an investigation after-hours, which meant he missed many more family functions than he did as a street cop. His absences had become more and more frequent, and it became obvious that there was no guarantee that time spent with his family would go uninterrupted. On top of that, there was always the constant fear for Alayna that, one day, he might not make it home.

Even so, Mac and Alayna still cared for each other and remained good friends. There was no animosity between them. They saw each other a few times a week when Mac would pick up Austin so he and his son could spend time together. After all, it is what it is, as the saying goes.

Mac placed the call and on the third ring, Alayna picked up. "Hi, Mac. I heard about the homicides at Rosalee's. How are you doing?" She sounded a bit out of breath, as if she had run to the phone.

"It's been a long day," Mac admitted. "We're still working on it, so I wanted to let Austin know I can't take him to the game. If you'd like to go with him, I can leave the tickets here at the PD and you can pick them up."

"No, that's okay. He enjoys going, but he enjoys going with you. That's something you guys like doing together."

"Yeah, I understand. I know it's short notice, but if your sister wants to go, I'll have them at the front desk for her and Nick. I hate to waste the tickets."

"That's a good idea. I'll give her a call. Be careful, okay, Mac?"

He could hear the concern in her voice. "I will. We have an idea who the suspect is, and O'Malley is typing up the search warrant for this guy's house now. Once the judge signs it, we're going to see if we can't grab him. I'll keep you posted."

"Sounds good. Bye, Mac."

Mac looked at the phone in his hand and gently put it back on the base. With a deep sigh, he picked up a folder from his desk and opened it to reveal the paperwork he'd amassed so far on the investigation.

· · · · ·

Brandon climbed into his unmarked police car and headed to Rockville to find out if the address they had for Dusty was a valid one. He had put the address in his phone's GPS system, and within a few minutes, arrived at the home. He parked across the street, and two doors down.

For the first half-hour he'd been watching the house, Brandon didn't see anyone go in or out. Then an Amazon truck stopped in front of the house. Brandon watched as the driver got out and dropped a package on the steps. He was in luck!

Brandon quickly got out of his car and met the Amazon driver at the truck before he could pull away. With the truck between Brandon and the house, no one would see them.

Brandon showed the driver his badge and police ID. The driver looked at him, wide-eyed.

"Who was that package for?" asked Brandon.

"I don't know. Somebody named Maria Castellano. Why? What did she do?"

"Did you ever deliver a package at that same house for a guy named Dusty Sampson?" Brandon asked.

"I think so, yeah. And if that's the guy I'm thinking of, I've talked to him a few times," the driver said.

Brandon held up the photo of Dusty Sampson. "Is this the guy that you were talking about?"

"Yeah, that's him. That's Dusty." The driver pointed to the picture that Brandon was holding in front of him.

"How do you know him?"

"I don't know him, except for the deliveries. He comes out to meet me a lot of times to grab the packages. He has said before that they've had porch pirates steal their packages, so someone is usually here when I drop them off. Most of the time it's him, like he's always home, or something. I'm kind of surprised he's not here now, actually."

"You think he still lives here?"

"I think so. I was here a couple days ago and talked to him. Why? What's going on?"

"Okay, thanks for your help. I appreciate it." Brandon ran back across the street and jumped into his car. The tires let out a chirp as he quickly pulled away from the curb and headed back to the PD. With all of their information pointing to that address, it certainly looked like Dusty was still living there.

·　　·　　·　　·　　·

Shortly after Investigator Powers returned to the CID office with his news, Investigator O'Malley walked in, waving the signed search warrant above his head. Mac glanced at the clock hanging on the wall and did a quick assessment. It had been twenty hours since the homicides.

While Powers was on his surveillance assignment and O'Malley had been meeting with the judge to get the warrant signed, Mac was busy on the phone, calling the WET team in again. He also added a few more uniformed officers to their team. Dusty Sampson was armed with a weapon and was therefore considered dangerous. They could use all the help they could get, and were not going to take chances with an armed subject who was on the run. Now they just needed to wait for the rest of the officers to come in.

Dusty had said in the Facebook messages that he had planned to rob a second place that night. It was getting late, so Mac was silently hoping that Dusty hadn't left the house yet to commit the next robbery. If luck was on their side, they would find their suspect at home.

Once they were all assembled, Mac ran a Google Maps search on the house in Rockville where they were hoping to find their suspect. They studied the picture of the home and the adjacent property, to get familiar with it. They then devised a plan where the members of the WET team would make entry into the home through the front door, while the remaining officers surrounded the house, in case Dusty tried to run out the back or jump out a window. If Dusty was in the house, they would find him.

It was a short ride to the house in Rockville, where they hoped to catch Dusty before he committed another robbery. Normally it would take about fifteen minutes, but the anticipation made it seem like a much longer trip. The night was quiet with very little traffic. Most people were at home, in the process of ending their day, getting ready for bed. Street lights gently reflected off the black van, as it pulled up in front of the house as quietly as a shark skimming through open waters. It was now twenty minutes to midnight, just over twenty-two hours since Dusty Sampson had killed two innocent people.

Each officer was wearing dark clothing and bullet-proof vests. They were all heavily laden with their tools of the trade; things like body cameras, tasers, guns and extra ammunition. The members of the WET team also carried flash bang grenades that were secured either in, or to, their clothing. One officer would carry a large black battering ram that would be used to knock down the front door and give them access to the house.

With well-practiced agility, the WET team members slid from their specialized van without making a sound in the night air. It took only seconds for them to surround the house. The cop with the battering ram swung the heavy metal bar into the front door, shattering the wood as if it were paper. Chunks of wood flew in every direction while the door knob fell in pieces to the floor. What was left of the door slammed against the interior wall with a loud crash.

The cops bolted into the house in single file, as if in a synchronized line dance, with half of them running up the stairs to search the second floor while the rest spread out to search the rooms on the first floor.

To the right of the front door was the living room. One lone figure rolled off the couch and lay prone on the floor. He lifted his chin to find the open barrel of an assault rifle only inches away from his nose. They had found Dusty Sampson.

CHAPTER THIRTEEN

Dusty had been drunk and out cold on the couch when he was awakened by a loud crash. He reached for the loaded handgun that was perched on his stomach as adrenalin propelled him off the couch and onto the floor. With a grunt, he landed on his stomach. He had no idea what was happening.

Dusty heard multiple voices yelling, "Police! Police!" All he could tell was that the voices seemed as if they were coming from near the front door. He heard what sounded like a small army stomping up the steps to the second floor, the noise drowned out by the thumping of his own heartbeat in his ears. He quickly threw the gun under the couch. Within seconds, as he turned his head, he saw a pair of combat-style boots stop in front of him. Dusty looked up to see the barrel of a rifle in front of his face pointed directly at him.

Dusty saw another set of boots approaching. Suddenly, his arms were wrenched behind his back and he felt the cold of the metal handcuffs against his wrists. It was happening so fast and the remnants of the Jameson's coursing through his blood stream had dulled his senses. It took Dusty a few moments to process the fact that he was under arrest.

A voice from somewhere above told him to get on his knees, so he shifted onto his side, curled into the fetal position and then tried to push himself onto his knees. Still drunk, Dusty was struggling to kneel without the use of his hands, so someone helped by pulling him up by the arm. From there, that person was helping him to stand. As he looked around, he saw an officer still pointing a gun in his direction, another disarming the handgun he'd thrown under the couch, and a third man was standing next to him. That man, Dusty surmised, must have been the one to help him off the floor. That guy was still holding onto his arm.

The cop that was next to him patted him down, but there was no need for that, since Dusty was wearing only boxers and a t-shirt. Did the cop really think he could hide a weapon under his shorts?

"Dusty Sampson," said the cop that had patted him down, "you're under arrest for the murder of Michael Schumacher and David Hamlin. You have the right to remain silent. Anything you say…"

"You don't need to tell me all that shit. I know my rights, man." Dusty glared at the cop.

"I'm sure you do, but I am going to read them to you anyway," continued Mac. He recited the Miranda rights as he led him by the arm, out the front door and down the sidewalk. Mac guided Dusty into the back seat of a police car that was parked at the curb and closed the door as soon as Dusty had both feet in.

Dusty watched from the side window as Jorge, and then Maria, both in pajamas, were escorted from the house in handcuffs to the waiting police cars. "Leave them alone," he shouted. "They had nothing to do with it!" With the windows rolled up, his voice did not carry outside the vehicle. When he realized no one was listening to him, Dusty started banging the window with his forehead.

Mac had been standing about six feet away when he heard the banging and immediately stepped towards the car. Mac threw open the door just as Dusty leaned towards the window, attempting to hit it again. If it wasn't for the seatbelt, Dusty would have fallen out of the car.

"Listen," said Mac. "I don't care if you want to give yourself a headache, but I do care if you break the window. If you don't knock it off, I'll have you take a seat in the grass and considering that it's wet from this evening's dew, I'm not sure you're going to like that. But it's your choice." Mac gave Dusty a stern look. When Dusty didn't answer but turned to face forward, Mac closed the door. He stood like a sentry next to the car with his arms folded across his chest.

Dusty continued to glare through the car windows as the officers went in and out of the house for the next half hour. They were carrying bags - some clear plastic and some brown paper - filled with God only knows what, out of the house and placing them in the large, black van.

Finally, the cop that had been standing outside the car got in the driver's seat while another cop got in the back seat next to Dusty. The one in the front seat started talking as he started the car.

"My name is Sergeant MacIntosh. That's Investigator Cooper sitting next to you. We're with the Gaithersburg Police Department."

"Yeah, I figured it was something like that," said Dusty. "Listen, I'm freezing. Can you get me some clothes?"

"Where are they?" asked Mac. He reached across the dashboard to turn up the heat.

"In a duffle bag by the couch. Can you get me some jeans and a shirt? Maybe socks and shoes, too."

"I'll be right back," Mac said as he opened the car door.

Once Mac returned with Dusty's clothes, they had him step out of the car and helped him get dressed.

Once he was settled in the back seat again, Dusty started talking. "Look, I didn't mean to kill those people last night. All the big guy had to do was give me the money. I just needed money. That's all it was. It sucks that it had to happen that way."

Mac caught Coop's eyes in the rear view mirror. "You're right about that."

·   ·   ·   ·   ·

Once they arrived at the police station, they brought Dusty into an interview room that was no bigger than a large closet. They led him to a plastic chair at a small table. Coop shackled one of his ankles to a large handcuff that was chained securely to a metal ring embedded in the floor. Mac watched from the doorway. Once the ankle shackle was in place, Coop unlocked the handcuffs from around Dusty's wrists, freeing his hands. With a length of chain stretching between the metal ring in the floor and the ankle shackle, Dusty could move but wouldn't be able to take more than a step.

"Do you want any coffee or water?" Coop asked Dusty.

"No, I'm good." Dusty said as he rubbed his wrists.

Coop closed the door to the interview room as he and Mac stepped into the hallway. "He's already confessed whether or not he realizes it, but I still want to talk to him and find out why he shot those people. I think I'll let him sit for a few minutes before we go in there, though. I'd like to watch him for a bit to see how he acts."

Mac and Coop went to the CID office to watch Dusty on the closed-circuit television screen as he sat by himself in the interview room. He appeared fidgety, running his hands through his hair and continuously bouncing his legs up and down.

After twenty minutes, Dusty put his head down on the table. Mac stood up and said, "Well, he's calmed down, so let's go see what he has to say. Are you ready, Coop?"

"Oh, yeah," answered Coop as he rubbed his hands together. "I'm definitely ready. I can't imagine what this guy has to say about shooting two people in cold blood, and trying to shoot at least one more."

Mac and Coop walked into the interview room and closed the door behind them. They each brought in a pad of paper, setting them on the table before they took their seats at the table opposite their suspect.

"Okay, Dusty. Again, I'm Sergeant MacIntosh, and this is Investigator Cooper. I'd like to read your rights to you again, but this time, I'm going to have you put your initials on this form next to each one as I read them to you. This will acknowledge that you understand your rights. Do you understand what I'm telling you?"

"Yeah, man. I told you already, I understand my rights. I'm not an idiot."

Ignoring the attitude from their suspect, Mac read through the Miranda Rights, and had Dusty write his initials next to each one listed on the form.

"We'd like to ask you a few questions. Do you know what it is we want to talk to you about?"

"Sure. You want to know why I shot those people at Rosalee's last night, right?" Dusty looked down at his hands.

"That's about the size of it," Coop said.

"I needed money, and I figured the fastest way to get money was to rob someplace. That's when I thought of the restaurant. I just went there to rob them but I don't know why I shot them. It just kind of happened. I'm not really sure why I shot them. I didn't mean to. The woman, I think her name is Natalie or something like that, she was begging me not to shoot her 'cause she has a kid. Then the gun jammed. The thing is, I just needed the money."

"Why did you pick that restaurant?" Mac asked.

"I used to work there, so I knew where they kept the money. You know, in the safe they have in the office. When do I get to make a phone call?" Dusty looked at Mac as if the thought had just occurred to him.

"If you want to call an attorney, you might want to wait a few hours," Mac said, looking at his watch. "Most people are still in bed right now and won't answer the phone, anyway."

"No," said Dusty. "I want to call my mother." He looked at the investigators, waiting for them to make fun of him for wanting to call his mommy. He had no way of knowing how common that request was.

"Sure, Dusty," Mac said. "If you can bear with us for just a couple more minutes to ask a few more questions, we'll be all set, and then you can call her. By then it'll be a more reasonable hour. Is that okay?"

"That's fine. She works late anyway, so she probably just went to bed a couple hours ago. Hey, can I get some coffee now?"

"I'll get it." Coop stood up, and left the room, returning a moment later with a white styrofoam cup of coffee, an apple spice doughnut on a paper plate, and a napkin. Dusty eagerly reached out his hands to take them.

"Where did you get the gun?" Mac continued.

"Some guy," Dusty answered as he took a bite of doughnut. "I don't really know him that well. I'm friends with his aunt, and she hooked me up with him." Dusty washed down the doughnut with a sip of coffee and cringed.

"Sorry about that," said Coop. "It might be a few hours old."

"So, this guy just gave you a gun, from the goodness of his heart?" Mac asked.

"No, I was supposed to pay him from the money I got from Rosalee's. I'm supposed to return the gun to him Sunday morning. I didn't buy it, I only borrowed it, but that still cost me $300. Is he going to get it back?"

Coop just looked at Dusty and tipped his head, with one eyebrow raised.

Dusty got the message and said, "Yeah, I didn't think so. He's going to be pissed at me when he finds out." Dusty took another large bite of the doughnut.

"What's his name?" Mac had his pen poised over the notepad, ready to write the answer.

Dusty barely chewed before swallowing. "Listen, I don't want to tell you all that. I did it, okay? I shot those people. The guy I got the gun from never knew what I wanted it for. His aunt doesn't know either. Leave them out of this, will you? And my roommates; they've got no idea what I was doing. They're like squeaky clean. Why did you have to arrest them? Are they okay?" Dusty was looking from Mac to Coop, his eyes showing concern as his thoughts turned to Jorge and Maria.

"They're fine," said Mac. "We have a couple of investigators talking to them now."

Dusty took another large bite of the doughnut, almost finishing it. "I'm serious, man. They did not know I was going to rob Rosalee's." Dusty was talking with his mouth full, occasionally sending a wet piece of doughnut onto the table. "You gotta let them go."

"Look, if what you're saying is true, they'll be released without being charged. No problem, okay?"

"Yeah, okay." Dusty let out a sigh of relief. "Can I call my mom now?"

"I'll tell you what," said Mac. "Give us five more minutes to wrap this up and then we'll take you to the phone. I just have a couple more questions."

"Fine." Dusty finished the doughnut, wiped his mouth with the back of his hands and then wiped his hands on his jeans. He ignored the napkin. "What do you want to know?"

"I still want to know the name of the guy that let you 'borrow' his gun." Mac wiggled his fingers to show quotation marks at the word "borrow."

"I told you. I don't want to tell you about him."

"What about the aunt? What's her name?" Mac pressed.

"Don't you get it? I'm not telling you that, either." Dusty scowled at Mac, his voice getting louder.

"Okay," said Coop, "how did you get away from the restaurant after you shot those people?"

"Listen, I'm not talking about other people, okay? I did it. You got me. You don't need to worry about him or anyone else."

"So, from that answer, it sounds like somebody helped you get away."

Dusty had a stricken look on his face as he realized his mistake. He just admitted to having a get-away driver.

Coop and Mac were used to taking turns playing the "good cop, bad cop" routine, and this time, Coop apparently was enjoying the opportunity to play the bad cop.

"Did you have someone drive you to Rosalee's, Dusty? Did they stick around to drive you away after you shot two people? Who was it? What about the guy that sold you the gun? How about giving us his name?" Coop leaned over the table on his elbows, getting in Dusty's face as much as the width of the table would allow.

"The thing is, Dusty, we already know." Coop stood up, curling his fingers on the table like a gorilla. "We have access to your Facebook Messenger account. We already know about Vince, who gave you the gun, Amy that set it up, and your friend that you call Shit Storm, who drove you to Rosalee's."

Dusty's face turned red as he yelled, "Then you don't need me to tell you anything, so shut the hell up. Don't ask me any more questions. I don't want to talk anymore. I want my phone call, and I want a lawyer. Now!" Dusty pounded the table with his fist, hard enough to knock over the empty styrofoam cup.

"Okay, Dusty. Give us just a minute and we'll set you up with your phone call." Mac said as he and Coop picked up their notepads and left the interview room, closing the door behind them.

Mac and Coop went back to the CID office. They told Brandon and Patrick about the interview with Dusty.

"That young man has quite the temper," observed Mac. "He admitted to the robbery and homicides, but that's about all he's saying. He's not offering up any details, just that he went in to commit a robbery and shot the two victims. That's it."

"He's not giving up any information on his co-defendants. He's pretty tight-lipped about them," added Coop.

"Well, let's get this guy processed and arraigned," said Mac with a sigh. "We've still got tons of paperwork to get to."

Mac and Coop returned to the interview room, where Dusty was waiting, his head resting on the small table. They removed the ankle shackle, but handcuffed him at the wrists again. After letting Dusty make a quick stop at the prisoner's bathroom, Mac and Coop escorted Dusty to the holding cell.

The cell was a square room, about the size of a small bedroom. Against one wall was a long wooden bench for the prisoners to sit on. On the opposite wall was a counter with a computer and a printer sitting on top. Attached by electrical cords to the computer was the digital fingerprint machine. A video camera hung from the ceiling above the counter.

On the way in, Coop hit the record button on the video system.

"We'll let you call your mom now and then we'll photograph and fingerprint you," explained Mac. The phone for the prisoner's use was hanging on the wall above the counter, out of reach of any prisoners when they were shackled to the bench.

"What's your mother's phone number, Dusty?" Coop was standing at the phone, ready to dial. As Dusty recited the number, Coop pushed the buttons and then gave the handset to Dusty. Coop and Mac stepped to the doorway, only a few feet away, to give Dusty the illusion of privacy.

"Yeah, Mom. It's me. I, um, got arrested. I'm in jail at the Gaithersburg Police Department." Dusty tried holding the phone tight to his shoulder and whispering, hoping no one could hear his conversation. Coop and Mac could hear every word he was telling his mother.

"I screwed up, Mom. Big time. I shot two people Friday night." He paused as his mother spoke.

"No, they're dead. I robbed Rosalee's 'cause I needed the money, and I shot them."

"I don't know, Mom, I don't know why I killed them. I just did, okay? Listen, can you get me a lawyer?"

"I know you don't have any money. I don't either." Dusty raised his voice, no longer trying to keep his conversation private.

Mac stepped closer. "Dusty, the Court will appoint an attorney for you. You don't have to worry about that if you or your Mom don't have the money."

"Yeah, Mom," Dusty said, "the cop just said the Court will get me an attorney so you don't have to worry about that."

"I know. I really screwed up this time, didn't I?" Dusty's voice cracked as it returned to a softer level. "Please don't cry, Mom. It'll be okay."

"Okay, Mom. I'll let you know if the judge sets bail. Bye." Dusty reached over the counter to hang up the phone. He looked at Mac and asked, "When do I get to see the judge?"

"It'll be a couple more hours yet because we have to write up the paperwork the judge will need for your arraignment," Mac explained.

Mac looked at his partner. "Coop, if you can get him processed with fingerprints and photographs, I'll start the paperwork."

"Sounds like a plan," said Coop. "Dusty, I'll have you take a seat while I get the process started."

He gently took Dusty by the arm, and led him the few feet to the bench. Just like in the interview room, Coop shackled Dusty's leg to a large ring embedded in the floor, but this time, he released only one wrist from the handcuff. He handcuffed the other wrist to the bench Dusty was sitting on.

Once Dusty was settled at the bench, Coop logged into the computer that was on the counter. He would add the pedigree and arrest information that is necessary to create the record when a person is fingerprinted.

After several minutes of typing, Coop unshackled Dusty and brought him to the computer. In the old days, they fingerprinted prisoners using an ink pad and paper card. Nowadays, the prints are taken digitally. Coop gently rolled Dusty's fingers across the electronic fingerprint reader, took his photo for the mug shot, and sat him back on the bench. He put the restraints back on Dusty's wrist and ankle.

Maria and Jorge had been interviewed and released. Just as Dusty had claimed, they didn't seem to know anything about his activities surrounding the robbery and murders at Rosalee's Restaurant.

·   ·   ·   ·   ·

An hour and a half later, Mac and Coop were escorting Dusty to the courthouse. As Mac drove, he offered a few suggestions to Dusty.

"I want you to be polite to the judge, okay? Make sure you're respectful and don't get mouthy with her. If she asks you a question, you need to answer, 'Yes, your honor; no, your honor.' Do you understand what I'm saying?"

"Yeah, I hear you." Dusty said softly.

Once they arrived at the courthouse, Dusty stood in front of Judge Evelyn Johannsen with Coop on one side, Mac on the other. She looked over the arrest paperwork, which consisted of the complaint informations that listed the charges as well as the affidavits from the witnesses. The Judge was already familiar with the case because she had signed the original search warrants and the arrest warrants. From her seat above them on the high bench, she informed Dusty that he was being charged with two counts of first degree murder and one count of first degree robbery. She set bail at $100,000 cash or $1 million bond.

Dusty shook his head. He knew there was no way his mother could post that much bail or bond. She didn't even have anything to use as collateral, since the house was a rental and her car was paid for, but fifteen years old.

"Judge, that's bullshit," Dusty yelled. "I don't have that kind of money. Can't you lower the bail so I can get out?"

Judge Johannsen pointed her finger at Dusty. "Young man, I will not tolerate that kind of language in my court. You will act like a gentleman or I'll have you removed. Do you understand me?"

"But Judge…"

Judge Johannsen cut him off, and repeated, "Do you understand me?"

Coop grabbed Dusty's upper arm and gave him a slight nudge. Understanding Coop's subtle message,

Dusty glared at the Judge but after a tense few seconds, he said, "Yes, your honor. I understand."

"Now," continued Judge Johannsen, "do you have an attorney, or would you like me to appoint one for you?"

"No, your honor. I don't have an attorney. Can you appoint one... please?" Coop looked towards Mac with a sideways glance and a subtle bob of his head, as if to say, *it looks like he got the message about showing respect to the judge.*

The Judge reached over the top of her bench with a business card in her hand. "Your attorney will be Thomas Weiss, and here's his information." Mac took the card and placed it in the back pocket of Dusty's jeans.

"Mr. Sampson, you're entitled to a preliminary hearing on these charges. I will set the date for next Monday at 1:00 PM. If you have any questions about those proceedings, I suggest you have your attorney explain."

As Judge Johannsen banged the gavel closing the arraignment, two court deputies stepped forward to escort Dusty out of the courtroom. He was now in their custody and would be taken to the Montgomery County Correctional Facility to await his trial.

Chapter Fourteen

It had been a long and emotionally draining time for Mac, Coop and the other members of the Gaithersburg Police Department. Two people had lost their lives during the robbery, but the suspect had been taken into custody within twenty-four hours and was currently being held in the Montgomery County Correctional Facility. Mac was proud of his team of investigators as well as the police officers that were involved.

But now it was time to head home, get some much-needed sleep, and come back on Monday morning to gather up as many of the loose ends that remained. There was still a lot of work ahead of them and more suspects to find and arrest.

Before he left the office, Mac had asked for a couple of patrol officers to search the side of the road along the route that Dusty had traveled to get home. Dusty had admitted during the interview to wearing a mask and gloves and throwing them out the car window, along with the sweatshirt he had worn.

Mac also asked for the State Police K9 dog to help with the search. Sometimes the K9s could sniff out things that might not be seen by people, especially if the items were hidden amongst the tall weeds.

If they could find any of these items, Mac would have them tested for Dusty's DNA to prove that they belonged to him.

Oftentimes, a sweatshirt will have a logo on it. If that were the case with Dusty's sweatshirt, Mac might be able to match it to the sweatshirt seen on the video from Rosalee's during the crime. Between the possible DNA match and the comparison with the video, they would be considered valuable and necessary evidence that could place Dusty at the scene of the crime.

The other investigators had already left but Mac decided to give Alayna a quick call before he also headed for home.

"Hi, how are you?" Alayna asked as soon as she picked up.

"Tired. I can't remember the last time I went this long without sleep, but we got the suspect, he confessed, we got him arraigned, and he's sitting in jail." Mac stifled a yawn.

"That's great! It sounds like that's where he belongs," said Alayna.

"Yeah, he had plans to rob Rosalee's on Friday, another place on Saturday, and a bank on Monday but thankfully, we caught him before he could hurt anyone else. I'm going to head home and grab a nap for a couple of hours. We all need to be able to come back in on Monday for a fresh start. We've still got other people we need to talk to and hopefully arrest, not to mention a ton of reports to write."

"Listen, I'll be making some fried chicken for dinner later," said Alayna. "If you'd like to swing by the house, I'll give you some. You can either eat it here or I'll fix you a to-go bag."

"That sounds great. I'll stop by at about six o'clock, is that okay?"

"That's perfect. I'll make sure it's ready by then."

"You're the best. Thanks, Alayna." Mac pushed the end call button, shut the door to the CID office behind him, and headed home.

· · · · ·

When Mac got home, he was too tired to shower. He took off his shirt and pants, and climbed into bed in his underclothes. He set his cell phone on the nightstand, as he thought about silencing it, but decided against that idea just in case Alayna needed to contact him, or God forbid, the PD. Within seconds of his head hitting the pillow, he was sound asleep.

After a few hours of sleep and a refreshing shower, Mac put on fresh clothes and headed out the door, on his way to his ex-wife's house - formerly his house - to have a bite to eat. Alayna was a great cook, no matter what was on the menu but her fried chicken had always been one of his favorites.

He pulled in the driveway, and had barely put the car in park when he saw Austin run out the front door to greet him.

"Hey, dad!" Austin said with a wave.

"Hi, Austin," Mac said as he gave his son a hug. He was grateful thirteen-year-old Austin still accepted a show of affection from his old man, although Mac would never say that to Austin and risk spoiling it. Mac knew that teenagers had a habit of doing exactly the opposite of what their parents approved of, especially when it involved public displays of affection in front of other kids.

Alayna had just finished making the fried chicken when he arrived. The house was filled with the wonderful scent of home cooking.

"Can you stay," asked Alayna, "or do you want me to wrap it up?"

"No, I can stay, if that's okay."

"Perfect. I've already set the table for three." Alayna pointed to the kitchen table with her tongs. "Why don't you grab the cornbread and put that on the table. Austin, if you can bring the lemonade, I'll get the chicken and we'll be all set."

Mac, Alayna and Austin sat around the table filling each other in on the happenings of the last few days. It was still early in the school year, so Austin told Mac about his classes, with gym being his favorite class, and math being his least favorite.

Alayna teased Austin by mentioning a certain girl in his class named Skylar that he seemed to like.

Austin denied that she was anything other than a girl in his class, but his blush gave it away. Mac and Alayna shared a smile over their son's discomfort.

Once they were all caught up on the family doings, Mac gave Alayna and Austin a basic rundown of what had happened at Rosalee's Restaurant, leaving out the gory details. Neither one of them needed to hear any of that. He explained how the pieces fell together and they were able to identify and arrest the suspect

"Wow, dad! I can't believe you caught the bad guy that quick!" Austin said. "That's awesome!"

"Well, remember Austin, it was a whole bunch of us, not just me."

By the time he left, Mac was feeling much better with a full stomach and a renewed sense of energy. Alayna had even managed to bake another of his favorites, a chocolate cake. She wrapped up the leftover cake so Mac could bring it to work in the morning.

CHAPTER FIFTEEN

After a good night's sleep, Mac rose early on Monday morning. He showered, shaved, fixed a blueberry smoothie for a quick breakfast and drove to the police department, with Alayna's cake in the seat next to him.

His mind was spinning as he went over the facts of the case and tried to plan the next steps in the investigation. They needed to find out more about Dusty's accomplices; the woman called Amy and her nephew Vince, who worked together to supply Dusty with the gun, and the friend called Shit Storm, who drove the get-away car.

He parked in the police parking lot and looked around as if in a daze. He'd been concentrating so hard on the investigation that he was surprised when he realized he'd already arrived at the PD. He hadn't been paying attention and didn't remember anything about the drive in to work. He shook his head and puffed out his cheeks as he blew out a breath of air. *Thank God the car knew where to go,* he thought.

Mac walked into the CID office and, knowing he would need a cup of coffee, headed straight for the coffee machine and inserted a K-cup pod. As it brewed, he let his thoughts return to the investigation. The night of the homicide, they had been able to obtain Dusty's home address from the laptop he'd used without having to get a warrant due to exigent circumstances. At that time, Dusty had been planning to rob another unnamed place the next night, so time was of the essence. However, the rule of exigent circumstances would not apply in the accomplices' cases, since they were not involved in the actual homicide. Their involvement ended with the exchange of the gun and the drive to Rosalee's, respectively. Still, they needed to find and arrest these people as soon as possible.

As long as it was quiet in the CID office, Mac took the opportunity to begin typing his report on the computer. As the unit sergeant and lead investigator on the case, Mac was responsible for writing the initial report that would be the summary of the investigation. It would tell the who, what, when, where, why and the how. It was always a good idea, Mac felt, to write the report while those specific details were still fresh in his mind, because the longer it was put off, the more he might forget some details. The other investigators and officers involved would be responsible for writing their own supplemental reports that outlined their involvement in the case.

Within an hour of Mac arriving at the police department, the other investigators arrived. Mac saved his document so that he could devote his attention to the next task at hand, working with his team to come up with a plan to find Dusty's accomplices.

Like Mac, the first thing Coop did was to head to the K-cup coffee machine. He added fresh water and made himself a cup of dark roast coffee. "Anyone else want a cup?" Mac, Powers and O'Malley all accepted Coop's offer.

With freshly made coffee in hand and a slice of chocolate cake in front of them, the investigators got down to business. "So, this is what I'm thinking," Mac began. "We need to find out where the accomplices live, which means we need to get search warrants to the judge as soon as possible to access the IP addresses from their Facebook pages. It would have been easier if Sampson had given us the names, but he was very closed-mouth about that. He refused to say anything at all about them."

"The good thing is that the search warrants are pretty much one-size-fits-all," Coop said. "I can type one up, and then just change the names and a bit of the description for each one so we can get their IP addresses, and from there, find out where they live. That'll save time, even if it's only a few minutes."

"That'll work. The problem is that it will take a couple of hours to get the warrants and then the IP addresses from the FBI, so I'd like to see if we can get security video from any of the local businesses in the area that might show the getaway car. If we're lucky, we'll get the license plate number from the video. If we can get that, then from there, we'll be able to find out Shit Storm's real name and his address from the department of motor vehicle records. We don't need search warrants for that, because it's public information.

"Coop, if you can start typing up the search warrants, I'm going to head out and see if I can find any videos. Brandon and Patrick, I'd like you to help me. It'll be quicker if we split up and hit the different businesses."

"Sounds like a plan, boss," answered Coop. "Say, if you find yourself near any doughnut shops, maybe you could bring back some doughnuts. I'm partial to headlights, myself."

Mac looked at the grin on Coop's face, and chuckled. His partner always had food on his mind.

After mentally drawing up a rough map of the area surrounding Rosalee's Restaurant, Mac, Brandon Powers and Patrick O'Malley divvied up the roads that were within a couple of blocks of the restaurant. Mac took roads on the east side of the restaurant, Brandon took the west, and Patrick covered the south. They got in their department-issued vehicles and headed to their assigned destinations.

Mac's first stop was the business next door to Rosalee's, where Shit Storm had parked to wait for Dusty. It was an urgent care medical facility. As Mac approached the front door, he looked up at the eaves. There, on the corners, were two video cameras. They appeared to be pointed towards the road, so they may have captured the car and hopefully, the license plate. *This could be my lucky day,* he thought.

Mac walked in and looked around the waiting room. It was filled with rows of hard plastic chairs, most of which were empty. He noticed a man sitting in the corner with a young child sitting on his lap. The child, glassy eyed and probably feverish, was looking without interest as the man leafed through an auto magazine. Across the room, a woman sat with a teenage girl next to her. Both were heavily engrossed in their cell phones. An older couple whispering in each other's ears, were the only other people in the waiting room.

Mac approached the front desk where a young woman in purple scrubs and light purple hair was busy typing on a computer on the other side of the counter. He introduced himself and held out his identification for her to see. "Good morning. My name is Sergeant Steve Macintosh, and I'm with the Gaithersburg Police Department. There was an incident next door on Saturday night..."

"Yes, I heard about that," interrupted the woman. "I heard two people were killed. How awful."

"That's right. I noticed you had a couple of cameras above the front door. I'm hoping you might have a security video."

"Yes, we do have security video. Let me get someone to cover the desk for a few minutes while I check it for you." The nurse picked up the phone and asked someone on the other end to come up front. "She should be right up and I can go back to check the video."

"Do you mind if I come with you? I'd like to see what video you might have."

"Sure, come with me." As another woman approached, the purple-haired nurse stepped from behind the counter. She held out her hand and said, "by the way, my name is Patty Mitchell and I'm the head nurse."

Mac shook her hand, saying, "nice to meet you." He followed as she led the way through a set of doors and towards the back of the building. She entered a room with a sign on the door that read "Private."

Patty sat at the only desk in the room and turned on the desktop computer while Mac slid a hard plastic chair, similar to the ones in the waiting room, towards the desk and sat beside her. As she logged into the video program, Mac explained that he needed to see the security footage starting at around midnight Saturday. They sat quietly, glued to the monitor as the video played.

"Go ahead and fast forward the video so we don't have to sit here and watch it play in real time. I'll let you know when you can slow it down," Mac suggested.

Patty did as she was told. She held one finger poised over the mouse so she could stop the fast forward motion in a split second. They both watched intently as the surveillance video sped by. Suddenly, a car appeared in the parking lot. The time on the video was 12:58 AM. Mac pointed to the screen, and said "That's it. Can you slow it down?"

Patty clicked the mouse and slowed the video. He leaned forward, closer to the computer screen, with his elbows on his knees. They both stared at the computer screen as the car pulled into the parking lot, curved to the right side of the screen and stopped next to the bushes. The car tripped the motion sensor light, which illuminated that area of the parking lot. Mac could clearly see the make and model of the car.

They watched as a man in a sweatshirt got out of the passenger side of the vehicle, hesitated for a moment, and then walked sideways through a small gap in the bushes. They let the video play, and at 1:10 AM, the man was seen running through the bushes towards the car. He was pulling on his sweatshirt, as if it was getting snagged on the branches. He yanked on the car door, jumped into the front seat on the passenger side, and pulled the door closed. After a few seconds, the car peeled out of the parking lot, turned left, and headed out of view.

"This is perfect," Mac said. "Can you rewind that and then enlarge it so I can see if the license plate shows up?"

"Absolutely!" said Patty. She seemed to be as excited about the discovery as Mac was. She clicked on a few buttons on the screen with the mouse, and the license plate came into view.

There it was, plain as day... a Maryland plate, number DHB822. Mac thumped his knee with his fist. "That's it. That's exactly what I was hoping for! Can you print a copy of that video for me?" Mac stood and pulled a thumb drive out of his pants pocket.

"You bet I can. I really hope you can catch this guy." Patty said. She plugged the USB into the computer and began the download.

"Well, to be honest, we've already arrested the guy that killed those people. He's sitting in jail, as we speak. Now we're trying to find the people that helped him, like the person that drove that car." Mac pointed to the computer screen.

"You've caught the killer already? That's incredible. I'm glad he's off the streets before he can hurt anyone else." Patty handed Mac the thumb drive, with the promise that she would be happy to help if he needed anything else.

Mac fairly raced to his car. He pulled out his phone and sent a group text to Patrick, Brandon and Coop. "Got great video from medical place next to Rosalee's. Have make, model and plate of vehicle."

Within seconds, his phone pinged with responses... "Perfect!" "Awesome!" and "Don't forget the doughnuts."

Chapter Sixteen

After a quick stop at the doughnut shop, Mac returned to the CID office. Coop let out a whoop as he looked up to see Mac come through the doorway. With a large grin, Coop gratefully relieved his boss of the box of doughnuts.

"How can you eat doughnuts after chocolate cake?" Mac asked.

"Easy. The cake was a couple of hours ago," Coop laughed. Mac shook his head.

Mac started his computer and logged into the program that police agencies use to access state records. He would be able to run the license plate and get the registered owner's legal name and address.

Mac was generally not fond of modern-day technology because he found it to be intimidating. However, at times like this, he was grateful for what it could do. He punched in the license plate number and within seconds, he had Shit Storm's information, including a copy of the photo on his driver's license. They now knew his real name was Seamus McCracken. He printed out the details, one copy for each investigator. It was easier for him than creating a digital copy and emailing the results to the others.

While Mac and Coop were working their magic on the computers, Investigators Brandon Powers and Patrick O'Malley returned to the police department. If necessary, they could scour the area around Rosalee's later on for additional video footage, but for now, they had what they needed.

"We're making progress," Mac said, "but just because we can now link these people together because of Dusty's Facebook messages, I don't think we have enough yet for an arrest. I agree these are the people we need to talk to, but we can't get them in here based on a hunch. We need to work on finding some hard evidence.

"I would like to start with McCracken and go after him first. His real name is Seamus McCracken and he has an extensive criminal history. The last time he got arrested was three years ago for possession of drugs. He served a couple of years for that and is now on parole. And because Parole does occasional spot checks on their parolees, his last known address listed in NCIC should be accurate. Turns out, it's right here in Gaithersburg and he lives in a low-income apartment building on King James Way. If we can get him in his car, I'd like to put a tail on him and see what we come up with."

"I can do that," volunteered Patrick. "I know right where that apartment building is. I can sit on the place, and if I see him coming or going in that car, I'll follow him and see where he goes."

"Great," said Mac. "Thanks, O'Malley. If you spot him, call it in. As part of the terms of his parole, we have the right to stop him and inspect the vehicle for anything that's in sight."

"You got it, boss." Patrick grabbed his portable radio and bullet-proof vest, and headed out the door.

$$\cdot \quad \cdot \quad \cdot \quad \cdot \quad \cdot$$

Patrick drove to the apartment building and slowly wound his way through the parking lot. He was looking for a tan, older model Toyota Camry with Maryland license plate, DHB822. As he carefully circled the lot, he saw a car matching that description parked near a side door to the building. As he drove past it, Patrick confirmed from the license plate that it was the vehicle he was looking for. He took one more lap around the building and found a parking spot near the suspect's vehicle. Now he would sit and wait.

It wasn't too long before a man came through the door of the building and headed towards the car that Patrick was watching. The man was glancing over both shoulders, as if he was checking out his surroundings. He stopped at the car, with one hand on the door handle and looked around again.

Patrick studied the man carefully and compared him to the photo that Mac had given him. It was a match. *Hmm, he's definitely acting nervous,* thought Patrick. *Let's see what he's up to.*

Patrick could hear as McCracken tried three times to start the car before it finally coughed to life. The suspect pulled out of his parking spot, leaving a blue cloud of smoke trailing behind, before Patrick started his own vehicle. The suspect turned right onto the roadway. Patrick let three cars get between them before he pulled out. He followed the Camry, but left at least three cars between them, hoping that McCracken wouldn't spot him.

Patrick picked up his cell phone and hit the button to auto-dial Mac's cell phone. "Hey, Mac. McCracken is in the Camry, and I'm following him, about three or four cars behind."

"That's great! Which way is he headed?" asked Mac.

"Hang on... I just got cut off," answered Patrick.

Patrick had been able to stay behind McCracken until a large delivery truck pulled in between them. He tried to coast to the side, his tires crossing the double yellow lines. He was hoping to spot the Camry, but it was no use. He was stuck behind the truck and now he'd lost the Camry.

"Oh, crap," said Patrick. "Nope. It's no good. I lost him. Damn!" Patrick slapped the steering wheel.

"That's alright," said Mac. "See if you can circle back towards the apartment. Maybe he'll head back there in a bit and if he does, you can stop him before he heads back into his apartment."

"Way ahead of you boss. I just turned around and I'm heading there now." Patrick hit the end call button. He was disappointed, but if luck was on his side, he'd be able to locate his quarry again.

Sure enough, within a few blocks, he spotted the Camry pulling out of a convenience store parking lot. *Looks like the luck of the Irish is with me today!* Patrick thought. He managed to speed up enough to weave his way through traffic and get directly behind the vehicle. This time, he would not lose sight of it.

Knowing that Mac would be able to hear him on the base radio in the CID office, Patrick keyed the microphone on his portable radio, and asked the county 911 dispatcher on the other end to send backup for a traffic stop. He gave his location and the description of McCracken's vehicle. Within a few moments, he heard sirens.

As soon as he saw a marked vehicle closing in on their location with lights and siren blazing, Patrick hit the red lights and siren on his own vehicle. Like a synchronized dance, four police cars and Patrick in his unmarked vehicle, grouped around the Camry and brought it to a stop. Patrick could see McCracken's face in the Camry's rear view mirror, his eyes the size of golf balls, as the police officers stormed his car. They ordered him onto the ground, handcuffed him, and put him in the back of one of the marked police cars.

Patrick leaned into the Camry and looked in the cup holders, the front seat and the back seat. Without a search warrant, he could only look for any kind of contraband or evidence of a crime, if it was out in the open. There was nothing there except a six pack of Budweiser beer that McCracken must have bought at the convenience store Patrick had seen him leaving. It was still cold, the condensation dripping down the sides of the bottles.

Patrick opened the door of the police car. "Mr. McCraken?"

"What the hell is going on? I didn't do nothing! You got no right to pull me over," he yelled.

"Actually, Mr. McCracken, we have a right to inspect your vehicle, as a term of your parole. But you're free to go."

"This is bullshit. I didn't do nothing wrong and you got no right to pull me over like this. I should sue your ass!" Patrick shut the door on McCracken's tirade. He turned to the closest police officer, held out his hand to shake, and said, "I appreciate your help. Thank you. You can uncuff him and let him go."

·　　·　　·　　·　　·

While Patrick was tailing McCracken, the other investigators were in the CID office, putting their minds to work.

Brandon had an idea. "Mac, while you and Coop are working on getting the warrants signed, I would like to go through the Facebook messages between Dusty and Amy. I really haven't had a chance to go through them yet, so I'm going to start reading them now to see what I can find."

Mac agreed that would be a great idea. He always thought it astonishing that people put into the written word what they oftentimes would not want other people to see or hear. Most people texted and messaged others as if it would be a private conversation, forgetting that technology made most things online permanent and sometimes public.

After a short while, Brandon announced that he had something. "Hey, guys. Wait until you hear this."

"What did you find?" Mac asked.

"About a month ago, there was an exchange on Facebook Messenger between Amy and Dusty. He was looking to get some drugs from Amy but she said she couldn't because her family would be coming over for 'Grandma Gardner's' sixty-fifth birthday. We already know that Amy and Vince are related - she's his aunt - so just for the hell of it, I took a guess and ran a criminal history check on 'Vincent Gardner' and I got a hit. He's been arrested quite a few times for things like burglary, petit larceny and grand larceny. He's got a couple of assault charges also. He's been in jail a few times, but never for any length of time. He's pled down on the couple of felony arrests he's gotten, so he hasn't seen much time at all. In fact, he's not even on parole or probation at this point. He must have one hell of a lawyer."

"Okay," said Mac, "but what makes you think that this guy is related to Amy? It might be the grandmother's last name but it doesn't mean it's Vince's."

"That's true, and it was a stab in the dark, but I took a chance and ran that name anyway. Interestingly enough, within the criminal history for this guy Gardner there's a woman named Amy Hoffman listed as one of his associates. The odds are that these people have got to be the same Amy and Vince that we're looking for so I looked up Amy Hoffman, and she also has an arrest record. The only thing I have on her, though, is an arrest from a few years ago for petit larceny. Her address is in Rockville, about a mile from where Dusty was staying with Jorge and Maria. I've emailed their mug shots and addresses to all of you."

"I think you might be onto something there," said Mac. "I've got McCracken's photo and address also. I've printed out a copy for each of you." Mac reached over the desks to pass out the papers.

"Hey, Mac, when are you going to jump on the technology train along with the rest of the world? You could have just emailed these photos instead of killing trees," joked Coop.

"Listen, I like putting my hands on the paper. I'm funny that way, I guess."

$$\cdot \quad \cdot \quad \cdot \quad \cdot \quad \cdot$$

By the time Patrick had returned to the police department, Mac and Coop had gotten the warrants for the IP addresses signed by the judge and then forwarded the paperwork to the FBI. Mac had marked the request "URGENT." The results had just been emailed back to them.

"I've got good news," Mac announced as he read his email. "The FBI just sent me the results of the IP addresses for Vince and Amy. It shows they're the same home addresses that are listed in the criminal histories that Brandon found. We've got proof that these are the people we're looking for. I think we've got enough for arrest warrants as well as search warrants."

Mac printed out the results from the FBI and handed the paper to Coop. "Now we've got something to take to the judge. If you can plug these addresses into the search warrants for Vince's and Amy's houses, I'll draw up the arrest warrants. Then I'll call Judge Johannsen and see if she's still available to sign them. Hopefully, she'll answer the phone but she's probably sick of us by now."

"Absolutely, boss. I'll get them ready toot-sweet," said Coop.

Brandon, with eyebrows raised, looked at Patrick and silently mouthed, "toot sweet?" Patrick shrugged his shoulders, a slight grin pulling at the corners of his mouth.

Just as Mac finished typing up the last arrest warrant, his cell phone rang. It was District Attorney Dennis Wozniak with news on a high-profile murder trial that he'd been prosecuting for the last couple of weeks.

A few months before, a local, well-known investment advisor named Carter Mills had beaten and killed his wife, Loretta. He had claimed that it was a horrible accident that took her life. He said that she had fallen in the shower, tragically hitting her head and that she'd died from the injuries. Mac, Coop and the Gaithersburg investigators were able to prove that he had, in fact, killed her. The case had gone to trial, and they had been awaiting a verdict from the jury.

"Hey, Mac," Dennis said. "The jury just came back with a verdict. I thought I'd let you know in case you wanted to go to court."

"Hell, yeah! I'll be there in twenty minutes. Don't let them start without me."

"You bet. I'll tell them to wait for you." Mac could hear the humor in Dennis' voice.

Even though DA Wozniak, as chief prosecutor for the County, always had a lot on his plate, he was known for his good-natured personality. He rarely showed the stress of his job even though he was considered a formidable force in the courtroom and was relentless when it came to prosecuting his cases. He had earned the respect of many of his colleagues within the judicial world.

As Mac hung up, he grabbed the paperwork from the printer and called to his partner. "Coop, let's go.

The DA just called to say that the jury came back with a verdict on the Mills case. We can sit in on that and then catch the judge afterwards to have her sign all the warrants.

They ran to Mac's department-issued Crown Victoria. Mac hit the speed dial for Judge Johannsen on his cell phone as Coop jumped into the driver's seat.

"Hi, Judge. This is Sergeant MacIntosh. I have the warrants from the Rosalee's homicides ready for your signature. Would you have a few minutes to sign them?"

"I was just getting ready to take the bench. I've received word that the jury reached a verdict in the Carter Mills case."

"Yes, I heard," said Mac. "I just got the call from DA Wozniak. We're heading there now to hear the verdict, so I thought, as long as we're going to be there, maybe you could sign the warrants when you're done."

"You can meet me in my chambers after the proceedings. Don't forget the supporting paperwork." She hung up before Mac could acknowledge that he had everything she would need.

Within fifteen minutes, Mac and Coop were walking at a near-running pace down the hall in the courthouse to the courtroom. It didn't take long for the verdict to be read, at which time, Mac and Coop brought the paperwork to the judge in her chambers.

·   ·   ·   ·   ·

With the signed warrants in hand, Mac and Coop returned to the CID office. On the way back, they had discussed how they would execute the warrants. They decided that the best idea would be to go after Amy Hoffman, Vince Gardner and Seamus "Shit Storm" McCracken at the same time. That way, one would not be able to tip off the others before the arrests could be made.

Mac called in the WET team. It would mean splitting up into three teams to apprehend the three different suspects and they would need as many people as they could get. For the two suspects in Rockville - Amy Hoffman and Vince Gardner - Mac had asked for help from the Rockville Police Department.

Mac and the officers on his team would go after Amy, while Coop would go with his team to arrest Vince. And because he'd already dealt with McCracken, Patrick and his team would go after him. They each grabbed the warrants they would need and headed to the door.

Chapter Seventeen

Each team, made up of investigators and officers, waited out of sight, about a block away from their respective targets' homes. Once they were all in position, each team quietly announced over the radio that they were ready. After the third team acknowledged their readiness, Mac keyed the microphone on his radio and said, "All units, go, go, go."

•   •   •   •   •

Patrick pounded on the door of McCracken's apartment. "Police, open up!" A few seconds later, McCracken opened the door a few inches, but failed to release the safety chain first. He recognized Patrick on the other side and slammed the door shut. Patrick turned the doorknob, opening the door as far as the chain would allow. McCracken hadn't thought to lock it. Patrick stepped aside and motioned to one of the officers. The officer used his shoulder to ram the door. The chain broke easily and the door swung wide open.

The officers stepped into the apartment, guns raised. They entered a living room with a threadbare couch, an armchair with a short leg that was propped up with a block of wood, and a wooden coffee table that had seen better days. McCracken was standing at the far end of the room, holding his hands on top of his head.

Patrick approached him and announced, "Seamus McCracken, you're under arrest for murder in the second degree and endangering the welfare of a child. Turn around, please."

As McCracken turned on his heel, he yelled over his shoulder to Patrick, "Murder? What are you talking about? I didn't kill nobody."

Patrick pulled McCracken's hands off his head, one at a time, and secured his wrists with a set of handcuffs. He led McCracken by the arm to Officer Brian Collins, who had been at the scene on the night of the homicides. Brian stood by McCracken's side as the officers looked around the apartment for anything that could be evidence.

Patrick took a quick look around the apartment. He spotted the laptop on the coffee table. Right next to the laptop, he also saw a set of keys. One key was clearly marked 'Toyota.'

"Are these the keys to your car, the Toyota Camry?" asked Patrick.

"Yeah, those are my keys. Why?"

Without answering the suspect's question, Patrick put the keys into a clear, plastic evidence bag. Then he placed the laptop and the power cord in another evidence bag.

Patrick pulled his cell phone from his pocket and called the private line to the county 911 dispatcher.

"Hey, Corinne. This is Investigator Patrick O'Malley with the Gaithersburg PD. Can you send a tow truck to my location?"

"Wait a minute," interrupted Seamus. "You're not going to tow my car, are you?"

"Okay, thanks. I appreciate it." O'Malley disconnected the call, and turned to Seamus. "Yes, I'm taking the car as evidence in a homicide."

Seamus shook his head and muttered, "I'm going to kill Dusty."

"What was that you said?" Patrick had heard him, but asked anyway.

"Nothing," Seamus answered quickly.

Nothing else seemed out of place, or of evidentiary value, but Patrick was not surprised. After all, the man was on parole and probably didn't want to have contraband laying around that could potentially send him back to prison.

Within a short time, the search was complete and the tow truck had arrived to tow the vehicle back to the PD so that the evidence technicians could analyze it.

Brian escorted the suspect to his police car and had him sit in the back seat. Patrick and the suspect, along with the other officers, drove back to the police department. McCracken was placed in an interview room and shackled to the floor, just as Dusty had been.

•　　•　　•　　•　　•

Mac and his team of officers from the Gaithersburg Police Department met up with a few officers from the Rockville Police department two blocks from Amy Hoffman's home. If Amy, who was bedridden, was alone in the house, they wouldn't need that many officers to take her into custody. However, there was no telling if anyone else was in the home and if so, whether or not they could be armed.

Mac and his team of officers walked up the steps to the front door of Amy Hoffman's house. Officer Eve Swanson, who had been at the scene the night of the homicides, was one of those officers from the Gaithersburg PD. Mac had specifically asked Eve to join them because sometimes it helped to have a female officer present when dealing with a female suspect.

Mac rapped on the door and shouted "Police. Open the door." After a moment's hesitation, he heard a woman's voice from inside saying, "Come in."

Mac and the officers entered the home. Just inside the door, they found a woman sitting up in a hospital bed, a clear plastic tube leading from a green oxygen tank anchored to the side of the bed, to her nose. The bed filled the small room.

With a wave of his hand, he motioned for the officers to search the home for other people.

Mac looked at the woman. "Amy Hoffman?" he asked.

"Yes, I'm Amy. What can I do for you, officer?" She closed her mouth and breathed the oxygen in through her nose.

"Is there anyone else in the home?" asked Mac.

"No, just me. What's going on?" Amy asked.

"Amy Hoffman," Mac explained, "you're under arrest for murder in the second degree."

"Murder? What in hell are you talking about? I can barely get my ass out of this bed, let alone murder someone."

"We have evidence that you helped supply Dusty Sampson with a gun. Your problem is that he used that gun to kill two people." Mac looked at the table next to Amy. It was the same kind of bedside table on wheels used in hospitals. He noticed the white powdery substance that was stretched into a long, thin line. Amy followed his eyes to the drugs on the table. She quickly said, "that's just sugar. I had a sugar doughnut a while ago and was just playing with the sugar that fell off the doughnut."

She raised her arm, as if to swipe the drugs away, but Mac reached across the bed and grabbed her arm before she could.

"Nope. That's not going to happen," Mac said as he held onto her wrist. He pulled a set of handcuffs from the back of his belt and secured one end to her wrist and the other end to the metal arm of the hospital bed. He then pulled the table away from her bed.

The officers returned to the living room and told Mac that they had completed the search, and no one else was in the home. Mac tipped his head and flicked his eyes toward the other side of the room, away from their suspect. The officers followed his direction. From there, they could still keep an eye on Amy but they were out of earshot as long as they whispered.

"Okay," said Mac, "this is a first for me. I've never arrested someone who was confined to a bed before. We've got to find a way to get her to the PD."

"We wouldn't be able to transport her in the police car, but what about an ambulance?" suggested Eve.

"Yeah, that should work. Good idea. I'll call dispatch and see if they can send an ambulance our way." Mac stepped onto the front porch and made the call, while the officers stayed in the house to watch their suspect.

"Hi, Corinne," Mac said to the county 911 dispatcher. "I've got a very overweight suspect that's pretty much confined to a hospital bed. Would you send an ambulance our way to transport the suspect back to the police department?... Thanks, I appreciate it." Mac disconnected the call.

He then called the sergeant on duty at the Gaithersburg Police Department. "Hey, Johnnie. This is Mac. I need to have an evidence technician process a scene in Rockville for me. We just arrested a suspect in the homicide case, but she's got what looks like drugs out in the open... we have a search warrant, but I'll have one of the officers stay behind and hold the scene anyway. I'm heading back to the PD with the suspect... Okay. Thanks, Johnnie."

As soon as the ambulance arrived, the medics brought in a stretcher with which to transport their patient-slash-suspect. Mac unlocked the handcuff from the railing of the bed.

Amy could walk very short distances with help, so she brought her legs over the side of her hospital bed and shuffled the few feet to the stretcher. She was wearing a well-worn house dress that had definitely seen better days. Eve took a blanket from the stretcher and placed it over Amy's shoulders to keep her warm on the trip to the police department.

"Thank you, officer," said Amy. "I appreciate it."

Once she and the oxygen tank were securely strapped to the stretcher, Mac handcuffed both of Amy's wrists to the side handles of the stretcher. Because of her size, it wasn't possible to handcuff her wrists together. She was loaded into the ambulance and taken to the police department.

After they had all arrived at the PD, it became obvious that the interview rooms were too small to fit a stretcher. The only other option was to bring her into the conference room. Once Mac pushed the conference table and chairs against the wall, the stretcher fit easily into the space. He left just enough room between the table and the wall so that he could slide in for the interview.

As an added precaution, the ambulance crew would stand by during the interview, just in case Amy suffered from any type of medical emergency.

·　　·　　·　　·　　·

Brandon Powers and Coop teamed up to take Vince Gardner into custody. They also brought additional officers from Gaithersburg and the Rockville Police with them, in case he proved to be difficult. He had a history of assault, so it was a possibility that he could get violent, which was something they'd rather avoid.

The team got into position, and as soon as they heard Mac on the radio yelling, "All units, go, go, go," the team stormed Vince's house. Brandon stood at the front door and yelled, "Police, open up!" He tried the door knob. The front door had been left unlocked, allowing them easy access. A female, who'd been sitting on the couch, jumped up as the police rushed in. She screamed, obviously frightened, and put her hand to her mouth. She backed away from the door, almost tripping over her feet.

"We're looking for Vincent Gardner. Is he here?" asked Powers. The other officers spread out to search the house.

With her hand still covering her mouth and tears starting to well in her eyes, the woman shook her head.

"Are you saying he's not here?" Powers asked.

All the woman could do was nod her head.

"Do you know where he is?"

She shook her head again.

If Gardner was hiding in the house, it was a security issue for the officers. They had their safety and the woman's safety to consider, as well as Gardner's.

From the front door, Powers heard a car door slam in the driveway. He looked out the window and spotted their suspect getting a package from the back seat. "Hey, guys. Get down here. Gardner just pulled up," he quietly radioed to the others.

Within seconds, a number of officers ran out the front door, their guns drawn as they ran towards their suspect. Powers stayed in the living room with the female, to make sure she didn't pull a weapon or try to escape.

Coop yelled as he ran down the front steps, "Vincent Gardner, stop right where you are. You're under arrest."

Gardner, who had been unaware that the police were at his home, was taken by surprise. He was walking on the sidewalk approaching the house when he saw the officers running out of the front door, towards him. His eyes were drawn from the cops that were running towards him to the officer who was yelling at him to stop. He dropped the grocery bag he'd been carrying. Something that sounded like glass breaking could be heard as the paper bag landed on the cement sidewalk.

Gardner turned away from the officers and took off on a run. He got as far as his car, but lost precious time as he struggled to open the car door. The cops were right on his tail. A tall, burly cop slammed Gardner into the side of the vehicle, holding him pinned to the car with one hand stretched across his back. The cop reached for the handcuffs hanging from the back of his belt, and tried to secure them onto Gardner's wrists, but Gardner was doing his best to pull away from him.

"What's your problem, man?" Gardner said. "What do you think you're doing?" He twisted away from the cop that was trying to handcuff him. He was able to break free and took off on a run. The officers sprinted after him. Gardner ran into the street. He looked over his shoulder to see that the cops had quickly closed the gap and were within a few feet of him. He slowed his pace, throwing his hands up to surrender. The cops surrounded him. He was brought to the ground and handcuffed.

"You're under arrest for criminal sale of a firearm." Coop said, as he helped Gardner to his feet. He recited the Miranda rights, while they led Gardner back to the house.

"Have a seat." Coop tugged on Gardner's elbow and he sat down with a grunt on the front steps.

From behind him, Gardner heard the screen door slam. Her voice barely above a whisper, the female asked, "Vinnie, what did you do?"

As he looked over his shoulder, he yelled, "shut the hell up, Jackie. These guys don't know what the frick they're talking about. I didn't do anything."

"Ma'am, I'm going to have to ask that you stay out here on the porch for a few minutes, but I have to ask you not to talk to Mr. Gardner. We have a search warrant to search the house, but I'll have the officers start with the living room. Once they're done, you can go back inside, as long as you stay out of the way in the living room."

Jackie nodded her head, signifying that she understood. She sat on the porch in an aluminum lawn chair, the old-fashioned kind with woven plastic webbing. It looked so worn and frayed, Coop hoped she wouldn't fall through the webbing.

The evidence technicians began scouring the house, while Coop thanked the Rockville Police that had come to assist. With the job done, they returned to their duties.

Coop had left his unmarked police car parked across the street at the curb. He escorted Gardner to the car, nudging past a crowd of neighbors who had gathered in the street to watch what was going on.

"What the hell are you all looking at?" Gardner snapped at them. No one answered him. They simply watched, whispering to each other, as he was placed in the back seat of the car.

Coop drove them to the police department as one of the Gaithersburg cops sat with Gardner in the back. As he pulled away from the curb, Coop saw Jackie crying on the front porch, her hand still covering her mouth.

Within minutes of each other, Amy Hoffman, Vince Gardner and Seamus "Shit Storm" McCracken had been taken into custody.

Chapter Eighteen

Mac decided it would be best to interview Amy Hoffman first. She could then be arraigned and transported to the jail, at which point, the ambulance crew that had been standing by with them would be relieved. They'd been tied up on this one call for a few hours, which, no doubt, could put a strain on the other ambulance crews that covered the medical calls that came in through the 911 center.

He asked Eve Swanson to join him as he talked to their suspect. The conference room was equipped with video equipment, which would record the interview.

As they entered the conference room, Steve introduced himself. "Ma'am, my name is Sergeant Steve MacIntosh and this is Officer Eve Swanson. We'd like to ask you a few questions, if you don't mind. First of all, how are you feeling? Are you doing okay? As you can see, the paramedics are standing by, just in case you need anything medically."

Mac and Eve sat down at the table facing their suspect while the medics sat in the chairs that had been pushed to the side. They were trying to be unobtrusive.

"I'm fine," Amy said, "but I'd like to know why you're charging me with murder. I haven't left my house in months. How could I kill someone?" Amy lifted both hands, palms up, looking for an answer.

"I understand you were able to provide Dusty Sampson with a gun," said Mac. "He used that gun to kill two people in a robbery at Rosalee's Restaurant."

"I didn't provide him with a gun. I never touched a gun. I don't like guns. What are you talking about? And even if I did, I didn't pull the trigger. How can I be charged with murder?"

"Do you know Vincent Gardner?" asked Mac.

"Yeah, I know Vince. He's my nephew. Are you going to tell me how in the hell I could possibly be charged with murder?" Amy looked from Mac to Eve and back again, looking for an answer.

"When's the last time you saw Dusty Sampson?" Mac was scribbling notes in the notepad that he'd brought with him.

"I saw him last Friday. Why?"

"And when's the last time you saw your nephew Vince?" Mac continued.

"That same day." Amy swiped at the perspiration that was dotting her forehead.

"Were they both at your house at the same time?"

"Yeah, I guess so." Amy looked puzzled, as if she was trying to figure out how much she should admit to.

"Why is that?" asked Mac. "Why were they both at your house at the same time?"

Amy hesitated before finally answering Mac's question. "Dusty wanted some pot. I occasionally use it myself, for pain, and I had a bit extra, so I was going to give some to Dusty. Vince just happened to stop by, that's all. It was just a coincidence." Mac noticed that Amy had a bit of a smirk as she answered.

"I see. And was it a coincidence that Vince just happened to bring a gun with him that Dusty had said he wanted to borrow?"

"I don't know anything about no gun," Amy raised her voice. "I keep telling you that, and you're not listening." Amy slapped the stretcher with her hand.

"Well, you see, Amy, we have the Facebook messages between you and Dusty where you're making the arrangements between the two of them to get Dusty a gun. You were the go-between, the person in the middle of Dusty and Vince, setting it all up."

As soon as Mac said they had the Facebook messages between her and Dusty, Amy's face went pale. She closed her mouth and began inhaling long pulls of oxygen through the tubes in her nose.

The paramedics had been sitting near the door, but as soon as they saw Amy's reaction, they both stood and rushed to her side. One medic pulled a blood pressure cuff from her medical bag and wrapped it around Amy's arm. It was a very tight fit. She then pulled the stethoscope from around her neck, putting one end of the stethoscope in her ears, the other end on the inside of Amy's elbow.

"Her BP is elevated, but it's within normal range. I think she's okay for now," the medic said.

The other medic checked the oxygen tank, to make sure Amy was getting sufficient oxygen. He offered Mac a thumbs up.

"Are you okay, Amy?"

"No. I'm done. I want to get out of here." She was drawing heavily from the oxygen tank.

"That's fine. I'll call the judge and see if we can't get you arraigned." Mac and Eve picked up their notepads and left the room, leaving the medics to stay with Amy.

Mac normally didn't stop an interview unless the defendant "lawyered up," but with Amy's medical conditions, he felt it best to wrap it up and get her to jail. At least there, they had medical personnel on staff that were better equipped to keep an eye on her. Besides, with the Facebook messages, Mac had what he needed. Her confession would have been a bonus, but was not necessary.

·　　·　　·　　·　　·

Investigator Patrick O'Malley and Officer Brian Collins entered the interview room where Seamus McCracken was being held. Patrick introduced himself and Brian.

"We want to talk to you about last Friday night. Can you tell us where you were at about midnight, Friday night into Saturday morning?" Patrick began.

"I was home. My ex-girlfriend dropped off our daughter and I was babysitting her."

"Did you leave your home at all that night?"

"No. I stayed home all night and played Candyland and read books with my daughter." Sweat was starting to build on Seamus' upper lip.

"How old is your daughter?"

"She's four." Seamus smiled at the thought of his daughter.

"Why do they call you 'Shit Storm'?" Brian asked.

"Because I have the worst luck. Everything I touch, everything I do, turns into a shit storm. Have you ever heard the expression, 'if it weren't for bad luck, I'd have no luck at all'? Well, that's my life in a nutshell."

"Do you know Dusty Sampson?" asked Patrick, switching subjects.

"Yeah, I know Dusty."

"How do you know Dusty?"

"Well, I was in prison a while back and I met him while we were both incarcerated." Seamus wiped the sweat off his upper lip, but there was sweat gathering at his hairline, also.

"Did you meet up with Dusty last Friday night?" Patrick asked.

"No, no I didn't. I told you, I was home with my daughter all night. We even read *Goodnight Moon* before she went to bed."

"So you're saying you didn't see Dusty Friday night. Are you sure?" Brian persisted.

"Look, man, I'm telling you, I didn't see him that night." Seamus was nervously drumming his fingertips on the table top.

"When's the last time you were at Rosalee's Restaurant, Seamus?"

"It's been months. I can't remember the last time, but it's been a long time." A drop of sweat traveled from Seamus' temple to his jawline.

Patrick leaned over the table towards Seamus. "What would you say if I told you that we know you drove Dusty to Rosalee's last Friday night?"

"I'd say you got the wrong information. I haven't been anywhere near that place in a long time. Listen, it's kind of hot in here. Can I get some water?"

Brian slipped out and quickly returned with a cold bottle of water. Patrick pressed on with the questions. "We also know that Dusty was planning to rob Rosalee's Restaurant Friday night. We know that he promised to give you $100 for the ride to Rosalee's that night," said Patrick. "You gave him a ride to Rosalee's and he shot two people. He killed two people, Seamus, after you gave him a ride. Did you know he was going to rob the place, Seamus?"

"God, no. I didn't know what he was going to do. I thought he was going to do a drug deal. I thought he was going to buy drugs. I swear to God, I didn't know he was going to rob the place."

McCracken grabbed the back of his head with both hands and let out a wail. He started crying uncontrollably. "I swear, I didn't know. I didn't even know he had a gun. I never would have taken him if I had known he was going to kill anyone. I swear. I had my daughter in the car. I never would have brought her if I had known what he was going to do. I wouldn't do anything to hurt my daughter."

Brian looked at Patrick and tipped his head to the side, raising an eyebrow. Patrick gave a subtle nod. They both seemed to come up with the same assessment, that McCracken was telling the truth, that he didn't know Dusty was going to rob the restaurant, let alone kill two people. However, McCracken had also just confessed to what they had already known, that he was Dusty's transportation to and from the scene of the crime.

It took several minutes for McCracken to calm down enough that they could continue with the interview.

Patrick wanted to change tactics, to try and keep McCracken calm for a bit. "So you don't live with your ex-girlfriend anymore? How long were you two together?"

McCracken sniffed before answering. "We never actually lived together, but we were basically off and on for about a year. She likes to mess around and I'm not into that. Just before she told me she was pregnant, I found out she'd been screwing around with a lot of other guys so I broke it off for good. Then she calls me and tells me that I was the father but I didn't believe her. I had to have a DNA test to prove that Emma really is my daughter. I guess all it took was one night with a bad condom."

"Why did you have your daughter with you, if you knew you were going to give Dusty a ride that late at night?"

"I didn't plan on having her that night. Like I said, my ex dropped her off so she could go out with some girlfriends. I told her I had plans, but she didn't want to hear it. She dropped a bag at the door, left Emma on the couch, and took off."

"Do you have a court order for visitation with Emma?" Brian asked.

"No, but I get her a couple times a week and a lot of weekends, whenever the ex has other things to do. It's okay. I don't mind spending time with her. Emma is a good kid."

"Just so you understand, you're also being charged with endangering the welfare of a child for having her in the car with you," Patrick clarified.

McCracken hung his head and nodded, almost imperceptibly. "What happens now? What will happen to my daughter?"

"We're going to finish up the paperwork and get you arraigned. It may be a while before you see your daughter, but that's between you and your ex."

Brian and Patrick left the room, closing the door behind them. They would continue to watch their prisoner from the security camera while they prepared the paperwork for his arraignment.

· · · · ·

Coop and Brandon entered the small room to interview Gardner. As they opened the door, Gardner looked up. The cold glare he gave the investigators told them what they were in store for. This would not be an easy interview.

As they took their seats, Brandon started with introductions. "My name is Investigator Powers, this is Investigator Cooper. We'd like to ask you a couple of questions, but before we start, would you like a cup of coffee? Maybe some water?"

Gardner stared at Brandon, his lips pinched together in a tight line. After a few moments, he said, "No. I'm good."

"If you decide you want something, just let us know. So, Vince, we want to talk to you about Dusty Sampson. How long have you known him?"

He leaned on his elbows at the table, maintaining the icy stare at the investigators. "I don't know."

"How did you meet him?" Brandon asked.

"I don't remember." Vince said.

"You met with Dusty at your Aunt Amy's house on Friday morning. Do you remember that?"

"Nope."

"You do remember your Aunt Amy, right?"

"Yep, I remember my Aunt Amy." Gardner leaned back in the chair and crossed his arms over his chest, trying to portray the illusion of being bored.

Coop then leaned over the table towards him, closing the gap. "And when you were at your Aunt Amy's house on Friday morning, you met up with Dusty. Do you recall that, Vince?"

"Nope, I don't recall that at all."

"Let me see if I can refresh your memory," said Coop. "Dusty Sampson wanted a gun. Your Aunt Amy gave you a call because she knew you had a gun that Dusty could use. She made the arrangements between you and Dusty for him to get him the gun. The agreement was that you provide the gun and Dusty would pay you $300 and your Aunt Amy would get $200 for acting as the middleman. That's a pretty lucrative business you got there, Vince. You let people borrow the gun for a few hundred bucks each time. How much money have you made off that gun, Vince?"

Vince didn't take the bait. He sat in front of Coop, not uttering a sound. On a rare occasion, he blinked.

"This is your chance to tell us if we've got the story wrong, Vince," said Coop. "What do you have to say for yourself, Vince?"

"I think you got it real wrong. I didn't give any gun to Dusty or anybody else," said Vince. "You guys need to go out and find some real criminals."

"Oh, I think you're a real criminal, Vince. You've been arrested before, haven't you?"

"Yeah, so what? I haven't been arrested in quite a while because I've been staying out of trouble. You might say I learned my lesson after my last arrest. I'm a model citizen nowadays, Investigator Cooper," Vince said with a smirk.

"A model citizen that runs a rent-a-gun business, you mean," Coop said. "Do you have any other guns, or just that one?"

"I don't know what you're talking about. I don't own any guns." Vince was sticking to his story.

"If you have any more guns, we'll find them, Vince. We're searching your home right now. We've got a team of cops looking through every inch of your home, as we speak."

Vince sat up straight in the chair. "You can't do that! You can't search my house without a search warrant, and I didn't see no search warrant," he yelled.

"Actually, Vince, we gave Jackie, your live-in girlfriend, the warrant. She can give us permission because she lives there. As a matter of fact, the house is rented in her name, so we had every right to give her the warrant."

Vince settled back in the chair, looking defeated. Angry, yet defeated.

"So," Coop said, "if you have any more guns, you might want to let us know now. That'll save us a lot of time, and your girlfriend will be able to get off the porch and go back in the house. I'm sure she doesn't like sitting outside while the whole neighborhood watches what's going on."

Coop and Powers quietly watched Vince, giving him a chance to mull it over.

"If you help us out and let us know if you have any other guns, we'll be sure to let the DA know that you're cooperating with us. Sometimes that kind of information goes a long way in figuring out any potential sentence," Coop offered.

"Are you serious? You guys are searching the house with Jackie there?" Vince finally said.

"Yes, we are. I'm not going to lie to you, man. She's sitting on the porch while our guys search the house. Unfortunately, the search team can be quite messy, too. They tend to pull your clothes and shit out of drawers and leave it all over the floor. They pull stuff from the closets and cupboards and leave it. It makes you wonder what kind of mess Jackie will be left with."

Finally, Vince said, "I have two guns. Dusty has the one, but there's another one in the bathroom ceiling."

"Which bathroom?" asked Brandon.

"The one upstairs. There's a vent in the ceiling that doesn't work, so I put the gun in the vent."

"Okay, thanks Vince. Like I said, we'll let the DA know you're cooperating. We appreciate it."

The man who had looked so cocky, so sure of himself at the start of the interview, was not so cocky now. As Coop and Powers left the interview room, Vince sat in the chair, his shoulders slumped, and his head down.

Coop immediately placed a call and let the search team know that there was a gun in the house and where to find it.

Now that the interviews were completed, Seamus and Vince were escorted into the lockup, one at a time, to be fingerprinted and photographed. They were then shackled to the benches to await the judge for arraignment. As they sat there, Seamus and Vince gave each other dirty looks, but that was the extent of their interaction. Neither one said a word to the other.

CHAPTER NINETEEN

It was now about 3:30 on Monday afternoon. Mac, Coop, O'Malley and Powers had found, arrested and interviewed all three suspects. Once they had typed up the affidavits, Mac placed yet another call to Judge Johannsen.

"Hi, Judge. This is Sergeant MacIntosh. We were able to arrest the three suspects today that we had been looking for. Would you have time to stop by the police department to do the arraignments?"

"I'm working in my chambers, Sergeant. Why don't you bring them to the courthouse?" the Judge suggested.

"I would, your honor, and I know it's not normally done this way, but one of our suspects is pretty much bedridden. She's very large, and we had to have an ambulance transport her from her house to the PD. She's still on a stretcher in our conference room. If you can come here, it would help us out so we don't have to transport her to the courthouse."

"In that case, Sergeant, I agree. It would be better if I went there. I'll see you in about a half hour." Mac heard the click of the disconnected phone call as the judge hung up.

His next call was to the 911 center to ask for another ambulance to come to the police department. They would need to transport Amy Hoffman to the jail once the arraignment was done.

The judge arrived at the police department at almost a half-hour on the dot. She walked into the CID office to let them know she was there, with her black judge's robe across her arm and a small leather briefcase in her hand.

"Gentlemen, we've seen a lot of each other the last few days," the Judge said with a smile.

They exchanged pleasantries for a few moments while the judge donned her robe and zipped it up. Her robe was like the television star Judge Judy's, with white lace around the collar.

"Judge, if you don't mind, I'd like to have Amy arraigned first. The ambulance arrived just a few minutes ago, so we can have her on her way to jail just as soon as you're done," Mac suggested.

"That's fine, Sergeant. Where are the other two suspects?"

"We've got them in the lockup." Mac pointed to the large television hanging on the wall in their office. It showed several split screens. One was a live view of the jail cell where Vince and Seamus were sitting shackled to the benches. Another screen showed the conference room with Amy and the ambulance attendants. They could see one of the ambulance attendants checking Amy's heart rate with a stethoscope. If a suspect was in an interview room and they had turned the video camera on, they would also have been visible on the television screen.

The Judge studied the videos of the suspects for a moment, and then said, "Okay, gentlemen. Let's get these people taken care of."

Judge Johannsen and the men from CID went into the conference room where Amy Hoffman was waiting. The Judge read the charges to the defendant and asked how she pleaded. Amy entered a not guilty plea. The Judge asked if she needed a lawyer and Amy agreed that she would need a lawyer. The Judge gave Amy the name of the court-appointed attorney. She pulled the attorney's business card from one of many she had in her briefcase and gave it to Amy. The judge finished the proceedings by setting bail at $100,000 cash or $250,000 bond.

As planned, the medics took Amy from the police department to the jail in the ambulance. Because she was still in custody, an officer also rode with Amy in the back of the ambulance.

Next, it was McCracken's turn to be arraigned. Coop and Patrick went into the lockup, removed Seamus' shackles and brought him in front of the Judge, who was still sitting at the table in the conference room. Just as with Amy, the Judge read the charges, to which Seamus entered a not guilty plea. The Judge also assigned a court-appointed attorney for Seamus, and she produced another business card from her briefcase. She set his bail at $100,000 cash or $250,000 bond. He was escorted back to the lockup, and their third suspect, Vince, was brought in front of the Judge for arraignment.

Once again, the charges were read to the defendant. Vince entered a not guilty plea, but he did not want a court-appointed attorney. "I have my own attorney," Vince said. The Judge set his bail at $75,000 cash or $150,000 bond.

The road patrol officers brought Seamus and Vince to the jail while Mac, Coop, Patrick and Brandon returned to the CID office to finish up their paperwork. Mac quickly typed up a press release and had Coop email it to the local news stations.

"That was one hell of a job you guys did and I'm damn proud of you," Mac said. "You worked your butts off and arrested all four people involved in the homicide. You did a great job."

"I think we should go to Jimmy's Saloon and celebrate," suggested Coop.

"I'll tell you what," Mac said. "I'll even buy the first round."

"Now there's an offer I can't refuse," Coop said, as he stood up and grabbed his suit coat from the back of his chair. He was the first one out the door, with Patrick, Brandon, and Mac following right behind.

•　　•　　•　　•　　•

Jimmy's Saloon was a popular hangout for cops, where they could relax and have a drink. Mac and Coop took their usual stools at the bar, while Brandon and Patrick headed to the pool table. This had become their regular routine.

Sandy, the bartender, was polishing the bar top with a towel. "Afternoon, gentlemen. What can I get you? The usual?"

Sandy had been the afternoon bartender for years, long enough to know what they would be having. Without waiting for an answer, she reached into the cooler, grabbed a Flying Dog for Mac and a Sam Adams for Coop, and plunked them on the bar in front of them.

"One of these days, Sandy, I'm going to order something different, just to keep you on your toes," laughed Coop. He took a long pull of his beer and set the bottle on the bar, ignoring the coaster that Sandy had set in front of him. "Ah, that tastes good."

"What time is it?" asked Coop.

Mac looked at his watch. "It's about 5:15."

"I have to be out of here by 6:30 so I can go home and take a shower. You know that nurse, Brandy, that I went out with last Saturday?"

"Oh, yeah. The nurse from the emergency room? How'd it go?"

"Great! We really hit it off. We've got another date tonight. I'm going to pick her up at 7:30 so we can go to the movies. We were supposed to go to dinner first, but I called and told her I'd be late, so we decided to just go to the movies. She understands what my schedule is like because her brother is a cop in Akron, Ohio."

"Sounds like she might be a keeper," Mac said, wiggling his eyebrows.

Coop pointed to the television hanging over the bar. "Check that out!"

As the news broadcaster was speaking, a banner reading 'Breaking news' streamed across the bottom of the screen. Sandy reached for the remote control to turn up the volume.

"... were arraigned this afternoon for their participation in the double homicide at Rosalee's Restaurant that occurred over the weekend. According to Sergeant MacIntosh of the Gaithersburg Criminal Investigations Division, Amy Hoffmann was charged with murder in the second degree and is now being held in the county jail on $100,000 cash or $250,000 bond. Her nephew, Vincent Gardner, was charged with criminal sale of a firearm and is being held on $75,000 cash or $150,000 bond. The third suspect, Seamus McCracken, was charged with murder second degree and endangering the welfare of a child. He is being held on $100,000 cash or $250,000 bond. This is breaking news, but we will be sure to keep you informed as more details develop."

"I sent out that media release just before we got here. Those people don't waste any time!" observed Mac. "I'm going to wait until at least tomorrow when I can talk to the Chief before I release any specific details to the media."

For the next hour, the investigators talked and laughed about various things, but none of it related to the double homicide at Rosalee's Restaurant. This was the time they sometimes used to unwind so they could leave the pressures of the job behind them, rather than bringing them home.

Coop, draining his beer, said, "Well, guys, it's been fun, but I've got a hot date tonight. I'll see you all in the morning." He stifled a yawn, as he got up from the stool.

"I'm going to be right behind you. We've been going non-stop for the last three days, and it's starting to catch up to me." He also covered a yawn with his hand.

Brandon and Patrick echoed the same, agreeing that they would also be going home, and probably heading to bed early.

CHAPTER TWENTY

It had been two months since Dusty Sampson killed two people in the robbery gone bad at Rosalee's Restaurant. After it happened, the restaurant had stayed closed for a week, partly as a tribute to those who died within their walls, but also to give the restaurant time while they cleaned the grisly scene. Someone had also constructed a small memorial of candles and flowers in front of the restaurant.

Unfortunately, most of the public had stayed away, probably spooked because of the gruesome crimes that had been committed there. The Gaithersburg police officers had made a point of eating at Rosalee's, not only on their meal breaks but also with their families, as a show of support. Slowly, the clientele was building up again, but it wasn't like it had been before the shootings.

Four people were in custody for the parts they played in the crime - Dusty Sampson, charged with robbery and two counts of murder; Amy Hoffman, charged with murder for arranging the gun that Dusty used in the homicides; Vince Gardner, Amy's nephew, who let Dusty borrow the gun; and Seamus "Shit Storm" McCracken, charged with murder and endangering the welfare of a child, for acting as the get-away driver while he had his four-year-old daughter in the car. All four defendants were sitting in jail, unable to make bail while they were awaiting trial.

Sergeant MacIntosh had been sitting at his desk when his phone rang. He picked it up and said hello.

"Hey, Mac. This is Dennis Wozniak. I just wanted to let you know that I had Dusty Sampson's case in front of the Grand Jury today and they've returned a ten-count indictment."

"Excellent! What is he being charged with?" Mac asked the District Attorney.

"He's charged with multiple counts of murder, attempted murder, robbery and weapon possession charges. He wasn't too happy when he found out, I can tell you that much."

"Most criminals that get caught aren't too happy," Mac agreed.

"From what his attorney said, he's not interested in a plea bargain. However, even if he changes his mind and pleads to a lesser charge, I'm still asking for a life term without the possibility of parole."

"That's only fair," said Mac. "To be honest, I don't really care what he pleads to, as long as he spends the rest of his miserable life in prison."

"I'll see to that," promised Dennis.

"What about the other three defendants?"

"I'm trying to work out some deals with them also, but it's slow going. I'll let you in on a little secret. The Federal government is stepping in. I don't know why, but they want to prosecute Dusty Sampson. If they can get the other three defendants to cooperate against him, they're willing to cut a deal with each of them. But don't say anything yet because that's not public information. We haven't worked out all the bugs yet, either."

"Hey, I won't say a word," said Mac. "But why are they going after Sampson?"

"I'm not really sure. They won't say, other than it was a cold-blooded killing. Maybe they want to make an example of him. I think every once in a while they zero in on a particularly heinous crime, and decide to prosecute. They're going for the death penalty."

"Really?" exclaimed Mac, more a statement than a question. "That's interesting how that can work. We don't have the death penalty here in Maryland, but if they prosecute and he's convicted, he can get the death penalty at the federal level."

"True, but he would have to serve his time that the judge sentenced him to on our charges before the Feds could execute him. The chances are excellent that he would die of old age while serving out his time at the state level before he ever saw the inside of a federal prison."

"Hmm, well, like I said, I don't care what the charges are, or even if they're state or federal, as long as he goes to prison for life and dies while he's in there. He's one character that should never walk the streets as a free man, ever again."

"I couldn't agree more," said Dennis.

· · · · ·

It had been four months since the homicides at Rosalee's Restaurant. Mac was at his desk in the CID office when a ping on his desktop computer alerted him to an email that had just arrived in his inbox. His eyes opened wide as he saw the subject line referenced Rosalee's and the return address was listed as the lab at the Maryland State Police headquarters.

Mac clicked on the email. They had determined that the sweatshirt, mask and gloves that had been recovered along the side of the road, belonged to Dusty. His DNA matched what was recovered from the articles.

Also according to the lab report, the beer bottles that had been recovered from Rosalee's parking lot on the night of the homicides had been tested for fingerprints, and the lab was able to get a match.

The fingerprints on both bottles belonged to a young man named Jonathan Clinton. Mac checked the criminal history that was sent along with the lab report and saw that his only arrest had been for a possession of marijuana charge two years before. It was time to talk to Mr. Clinton, to find out if he had anything to do with the incident.

Hoping the two-year-old phone number listed on the report was still valid, Mac dialed the number. After several rings, Mac was just about to hang up the phone when a voice offered a hesitant "hello?"

"Is this Jonathan Clinton?" asked Mac.

"Yeah, this is Jon."

"Jon, this is Sergeant MacIntosh with the Gaithersburg Police Department. If you have a minute, I'd like to ask you a couple of questions."

"No problem. I kinda figured you'd be calling me at some point, although I thought it would have been before now."

"Why is that?" asked Mac.

"I heard about the two guys getting killed at Rosalee's and I knew I left a couple of beer bottles outside the restaurant that night. I figured it was only a matter of time before they came back to me."

"Well, you're right about that. I got the lab report earlier today, and it showed that your fingerprints were on the bottles. Can you tell me what you were doing there that night?"

"Yeah, I was with my friend Kenny Jacobs. He's going out with the bartender, Desiree Federman, so he went inside for a bit to see her. I don't like hanging out with that many people around because it's always too friggin' loud for me. So I bought a couple of beers and sat at the picnic table in the back while I waited for Kenny. After about an hour, he came out, and we left."

"Okay, Jon. I appreciate your time. We had talked to Desiree and the other employees who'd been working that night, and she told us about Kenny stopping in to see her that night, and that you had given him a ride. We just needed to double-check the story, but I don't anticipate having to contact you again about this. Thank you, and have a good rest of your day." Mac disconnected the call.

The phone call to Jon was merely a formality, since Kenny and Desiree had already told the investigators about him. It was one more thing Mac was able to cross off his list of things to do.

CHAPTER TWENTY-ONE

Over the course of the next several months, District Attorney Dennis Wozniak was in communication with the defendant's attorneys and the federal prosecutors to try to cut a deal with all four defendants. None of their attorneys recommended going to trial, and three of the four defendants agreed.

Seamus was the only one who wanted his case heard and insisted on going to trial. He claimed that Dusty forced him at gunpoint to take part, and he wanted to tell his side of the story in a court of law.

Vincent Gardner was the first defendant to be sentenced. He had pled in June to criminal sale of a firearm and was sentenced the following month to two to four years in prison.

In May, Amy Hoffman went before Judge Johannsen and pleaded guilty to the reduced charge of first degree robbery, rather than the murder charges.

The media had been following the story since the incident happened the previous September and were present when each of the defendants entered a plea in

Court. After Amy's court appearance, the reporters met with DA Wozniak in a press conference immediately following the proceedings.

He explained why her charges had been reduced from murder to robbery. "In exchange for her cooperation in prosecuting Dusty Sampson," he said, "we agreed the charges and the sentence would be reduced. She had admitted to acting as the connection between Dusty and her nephew, Vince Gardner, who provided the gun that Dusty would use to kill two people. Although she didn't know *where* Dusty would commit the robbery, she knew he intended to commit a robbery, and that's what he wanted the gun for. She knew also that she would share in the proceeds of that robbery, in exchange for setting up Dusty with the gun. In addition, part of her plea agreement was that she would cooperate against the planned federal death penalty prosecution of Dusty Sampson.

"It is for these reasons that the people allowed Amy Hoffman to plead guilty to robbery in the first degree," explained DA Wozniak.

·　　·　　·　　·　　·

Amy appeared before Judge Johannsen in August for her sentencing. The court security officer brought her into the courtroom in a wheelchair, an oxygen tank strapped to the back. A clear plastic tube ran from the tank to her nose.

DA Wozniak took a moment to speak before the Judge announced the sentence. "Amy Hoffman was an active participant in the crimes committed that night. She played a significant role," he said. "She may not have been present at the restaurant that night and she may not have pulled the trigger, but she provided the gun to Dusty Sampson."

Because of her willing involvement in the robbery, he was asking for the maximum sentence allowed by law, fifteen years in prison.

Natalie Petrenko, one of two survivors, was also present in the courtroom for Amy's sentencing. She had asked to be given the chance to read what's known as a victim impact statement in the hopes that her words might have an influence on the sentence. She stood at a podium facing the Judge and read from the paper she held in her quivering hands. "No matter how hard I try not to think about what happened that night, the anger I have for the people responsible for this horrific tragedy seeps in anyway. So does the horror of that night and the sadness that followed." Natalie stopped, drew a breath, and looked directly at Amy. "Ms. Hoffman, you could have honestly prevented all of this had you not given a gun to a person who is pure evil. You could have done something to prevent it, even after he left your house with the gun, and yet you did nothing."

After the prosecution and Natalie spoke to the courtroom, it was the defense attorney's turn. Attorney Jacob Schultz stood at the podium and addressed the court. He explained that Amy Hoffman has lived a tough life since she was a child.

"Although the family and victims of this case now live in hell," he explained, "Amy Hoffman has lived in hell from the time that she was seven years old. Her stepfather is the father of her children. She was the victim of constant abuse that caused severe depression and post-traumatic stress, and that set the stage for her to make some poor choices and to be manipulated. She turned to drugs to find relief from the pain of depression and the pain from her health issues. Those drugs only amplified her depression and PTSD, enough so that she could never make sound decisions."

After her attorney finished speaking, Judge Johannsen asked Amy if she would like to speak. Amy simply shook her head and remained quiet in the wheelchair. Judge Johannsen sentenced her to the fifteen years in prison that the District Attorney had recommended.

"But because of her health," the Judge said, "Ms. Hoffman will probably never be released from prison." Little did she know how true her words would be, when Amy passed away from her health issues after thirty-three months in prison.

· · · · ·

Seamus McCracken was the last of Dusty's co-defendants to be sentenced for his role as the driver.

He had brought Dusty to and from the scene of the crime. He had been in jail for thirteen months and had not seen his daughter, Emma, in all that time. His ex-girlfriend had moved on and found another boyfriend to watch Seamus' daughter while she went dancing at the clubs. She wouldn't answer his phone calls and had never come to the jail to see him.

Seamus had asked his court-appointed attorney to intervene, to force his ex to bring Emma to see him. There wasn't much the attorney could do. Seamus needed a family court attorney, not a criminal attorney. The attorney did, however, offer an opinion on the matter. Until the child is older and could understand, it would be a good idea to "let sleeping dogs lie." Seamus apparently listened to the attorney's suggestion that it wasn't a good idea in the long run to pursue the matter. Did he really want his little girl to see him in prison behind bars? Seamus decided to let it drop. Prison was no place for a now-five-year-old, anyway.

The Grand Jury had indicted Seamus on two counts of murder in the second degree, one count of robbery in the first degree, two counts of criminal possession of a weapon and endangering the welfare of a child. Still, he was adamant that Dusty had coerced him at gunpoint to drive to Rosalee's Restaurant the night of the robbery and murders. No matter how many times his attorney told him he'd already confessed to the police, and no part of that confession involved being held at gunpoint, Seamus did not want to hear it. He told his attorney that he had lied during the confession, that he was telling the truth now. He was hoping he could get away with the current lie.

His trial was set to begin with jury selection on July 12th. That same morning, Seamus finally listened to his attorney and changed his mind. He accepted a plea to robbery to avoid the remaining charges. He would not be going to trial after all.

The court officers brought Seamus in front of Judge Johannsen in December for sentencing. As with Amy Hoffman, Natalie Petrenko asked to give a victim's statement.

Natalie spoke to the courtroom from the same podium as before. She tearfully admitted she still feels guilt that she survived while a friend and her fiance - Schumacher and Hamlin - didn't. And the fact that McCracken was too scared to report the killer when he had the chance, after the police had stopped him the next day, makes her angry.

"Hallucinations, depression, horrific nightmares: those are the scars that I carry from that night. Your decisions that night make you a coward," she said as she looked directly at Seamus. "In my eyes, you are just as guilty as the monster who pulled the trigger," Natalie concluded. "The only thing you feel sorry for is yourself."

The next person who had asked to speak at the sentencing was Maria Schumacher, whose son, Michael, was the manager when he was killed that night. After listening to Natalie, it took Maria a moment to compose herself. She stood at the podium, quietly looking at the papers she had placed on top. With a deep breath, she began.

"When you killed my son, you not only took him from my husband and me, but you also took a father from his two kids. Now, my husband and I are raising Mike's kids, but my husband is disabled, so it's difficult. I could always depend on Mike to help, but I can't do that anymore.

"The holidays will always be especially hard now. Mike was always around to help with things like the Thanksgiving dinner. We would spend two or three hours in the kitchen cooking together, but this past holiday season, instead of cooking, I cried for those two or three hours."

After listening to the victim's statements, Judge Johannsen declared that she was ready to sentence Seamus for his involvement in the robbery and homicides.

"If you hadn't given Mr. Sampson a ride, none of us would be here," the Judge told Seamus. "That's what tortures them. And from now on, that's what should torture you. You did not tell the police about your involvement that night, even after you were pulled over the next day. You are hereby sentenced to spend the next fifteen years in prison."

With the pounding of Judge Johannsen's gavel on the bench, the case against Seamus "Shit Storm" McCracken came to a close.

Sergeant MacIntosh, Coop, Brandon Powers and Patrick O'Malley had tried to make as many court appearances as they were able when any of the defendants were being sentenced. It was not only a matter of closure for the victims, it was also closure for them. It helped seeing that all their hard work on the investigation had paid off, and gave them the satisfaction of seeing the bad guys go to jail.

Now that Vincent Gardner, Amy Hoffman and Seamus McCracken were sentenced, there was only one left. Dusty Sampson. The investigators were looking forward to seeing him get sentenced.

CHAPTER TWENTY-TWO

Dusty Sampson was not doing well in jail. He had been incarcerated for only a couple of days when he tried to pick a fight with another inmate in the enclosed common area of their housing section. The other inmate wanted no part of it and backed away from Dusty with his hands in the air, in a show of surrender. Although no physical altercation was taking place, it was enough to catch the eyes of the guards who were standing nearby.

The guards were used to the occasional disagreement between inmates and were trained on how to quickly diffuse any situation before it turned into a physical fight. They began walking towards Dusty with the intention of simply calming him down, but Dusty saw their approach as a threat. The other inmates sensed an altercation was imminent, and watched with interest as the events unfolded.

Before the guards had a chance to talk to him, Dusty charged the closest guard and knocked him down. He turned to the second guard and punched him in the jaw. Within moments, at least a half-dozen other guards came out of nowhere and joined in the fracas.

Dusty took off and was running free, dodging between the bolted-down tables and chairs, like a rabbit in the wild. He was laughing, almost taunting the guards. Most of the other inmates had been sitting at the tables either playing cards or watching television, but as Dusty ran between them, the inmates left their cards on the table and scrambled to the opposite side of the open area. It was a better place to watch the goings-on without getting involved. They began hooting and hollering, cheering Dusty on, even though they knew from experience what would happen to Dusty when the guards caught him.

The cacophony of voices only fueled the fire for Dusty as he weaved between the tables, keeping just one step ahead of the guards.

Finally, in a well-orchestrated act, the guards surrounded Dusty and penned him into one small area. They moved inward, tightening their circle until Dusty had nowhere to run. Still, he ran toward a guard, trying to break through their stronghold.

The guard he ran towards was ready for him and fired off a long stream of pepper spray that landed squarely in Dusty's face. Dusty fell to the floor, yelling, screaming, coughing hard, and unable to see because his eyes flooded with tears from the noxious fumes.

Now that he was on the ground, the guards could subdue him. They placed him in handcuffs. Still, he continued to struggle and squirm. It was a futile effort.

The guards lifted Dusty off the floor by the arms as the inmates continued to jeer. He answered back with a few choice words of his own for the guards and his fellow inmates. Dusty was quickly escorted out of the common area and brought to the medical wing to have his eyes flushed with saline solution.

After visiting the medical wing, they brought Dusty to a cell in solitary confinement, or "the box" as it was commonly called. With this form of disciplinary action, he would be allowed out for only one hour a day for exercise. He would not see the other inmates in the general population, he would not go to the cafeteria, but he would get his meals brought to him on a tray and he would sleep on a thin mattress on the floor. He would not pass 'Go,' he would not collect $200.

· · · · ·

District Attorney Dennis Wozniak had brought the case against Dusty Sampson in front of the Grand Jury in November, two months after he committed the crimes.

The Grand Jury indicted Dusty on multiple counts of first- and second degree murder, attempted murder, robbery and criminal possession of a weapon, for a total of ten charges. In some states, it could mean a death penalty, but in the state of Maryland, where there is no death penalty, he would most likely be sentenced to the maximum penalty of life in prison without the possibility of parole.

A week after being indicted, the jail officers brought Dusty before Judge Johannsen to be arraigned on the charges brought by the Grand Jury.

"Mr. Sampson, how do you plead to the charges?" asked Judge Johannsen.

Dusty looked the Judge in the eye, tossed his head back and said, "Doesn't matter. I don't give a shit." His attorney, Tom Weiss, quickly told Dusty to stop being disrespectful to the Judge, and entered a not guilty plea on his defendant's behalf.

"Mr. Sampson, we will set your case down for trial. My clerk will be in touch with your attorney to set the date for the trial." With a bang of the gavel, the arraignment was over, and they escorted Dusty back to prison and back to the box.

•　　•　　•　　•　　•

Dusty's defense attorney, Thomas Weiss, was doing his job for his client by going to court and claiming that the time spent in solitary confinement was causing a deterioration in Dusty's mental condition. To make matters worse, he said, Dusty was going through drug and alcohol withdrawal.

Judge Johannsen pointed out that the time in solitary confinement was a direct result of Dusty's own actions and, as a county criminal court judge, she had no control over the jail's disciplinary policies. Simply put, if Dusty continued to act out, he should expect to be punished, and it was his own doing. The Judge also let Weiss know that he would be welcomed to appeal the jail's punishment, but that would go to a different court, specifically, the State Supreme Court.

However, after hearing what Dusty's defense attorney had to say about his client's emotional well-being, Judge Johannsen ordered a mental evaluation. The psychiatrist met with Dusty and determined that he was mentally competent. He was a very angry young man, but he was capable of understanding the charges lodged against him.

For the next several months, Weiss would continue to go to bat for Dusty, arguing that he had become suicidal and that sanctioning a mentally ill inmate to spend that much time in solitary confinement was "unconscionably unfair."

Dusty, regardless of what his attorney tried to tell him, failed to realize that being put in solitary confinement was not the result of his mental state, but was a punishment for his unacceptable behavior. Almost to prove the point, Dusty more than once threw urine and toilet water at a guard who was picking up his dinner tray. And every time he acted out, it only added more and more time to his solitary confinement. Dusty would spend the next seven months in the box, for the sake and safety of everyone concerned, while his court case dragged on.

Still, Weiss pressed on, trying to approach the angle that Dusty's mental health and drug and alcohol addictions were contributing factors towards his behavior on the night of the murders, as evidenced by his behavior while in prison.

Weiss visited Dusty in prison several times and explained to him it would be better to plead to only one or two charges, and hope for the slim chance of getting a reduced sentence. If he pleaded to the full indictment, he would be in prison for life. No question about it.

No matter how hard he tried, Weiss could not get his client to accept that a plea agreement was the best-case scenario. Nonetheless, during his many court appearances with Judge Johannsen on Dusty's behalf, an exasperated Weiss maintained that Dusty's time spent in the box, coupled with his previous drug and alcohol abuse, prevented Dusty from understanding any plea agreements that the district attorney offered.

As far as DA Dennis Wozniak was concerned, Dusty could understand the charges. The psychiatrist who evaluated Dusty had confirmed it. But, for whatever reason, Dusty had made up his mind that he would not accept a plea agreement.

After all this time listening to Dusty's attorney allege repeatedly that his client didn't understand, the DA had had enough. If Dusty didn't want to work with his own defense counsel and the district attorney's office, then Dennis wouldn't work to reduce the charges, either. Enough was enough. The indictment would stand, and there would be no reduction in charges. He could either plead to the charges brought by the indictment, or he could go to trial.

To complicate things even further, Weiss was informed in April that the federal government was pursuing their own charges against Dusty. He had just been indicted on federal charges of murder and robbery, as well as eight special findings, including the intentional killing of more than one person. Where the state of Maryland did not have a death penalty, the federal government did. Dusty could very well go to the electric chair if found guilty on the federal charges. And the Feds had told Weiss they were going for the death penalty.

In April, Dusty was once again brought to court, only this time it was federal court and in front of Federal Judge Mortimer Abrahms. The Judge arraigned him on the federal charges and entered a mandatory not guilty plea with the help of a newly assigned federal defense attorney, Louis Perkins.

Shortly after the federal arraignment, Weiss went to see Dusty in prison. "Listen, you need to pay attention to what I'm telling you. We're not playing games here. The DA has already pulled the possibility of any plea agreements on the state charges, so the worst you'll get on them is life in prison. But the feds aren't messing around, Dusty. They're asking for the death penalty!"

"I thought you were going to convince them it was the drugs and alcohol that messed me up? It wasn't my fault."

"No, I wasn't able to. Remember, the evaluation with the psychiatrist showed that you are capable of understanding the charges and assisting in your own defense. Besides, I told you two weeks ago that DA Wozniak pulled the plug on that. He's letting the indictment stand because you wouldn't even consider a plea agreement. You will have to either plead to those charges, or go to trial on them. There won't be any more offers. That ship has sailed, Dusty."

"Fine," Dusty said. "I don't give a shit one way or another. It's not like I'll ever get out of prison, anyway, so I'll plead to whatever charges he wants me to."

"At this point, I think that's the best way, Dusty," Weiss advised. "The DA will not budge on the charges. He's already said so, and he won't take that back. Too much time has passed, waiting for you to make up your mind."

"Can you still ask for a lighter sentence? Maybe he'll go light on the sentence if I plead to all the charges."

"I doubt it, Dusty. That's what the plea agreement was going to do. The only thing I can try to do now is see if the Feds will take the death penalty off the table if you plea to all ten state charges. If you can get life in prison without the possibility of parole on the state charges, they may be willing to work with us at that point."

"Fine," said Dusty. "Do that. Get them to forget about the death penalty, and I'll go to prison for life."

Weiss hesitated a moment and then said, "I'll ask, but I can't promise it will work. I'll ask, though. I will, Dusty. I'll try." With that, he signaled the guard that he would be leaving and his client can be returned to his cell.

Chapter Twenty-Three

Just as Dusty's attorney, Tom Weiss, had predicted, District Attorney Dennis Wozniak was not willing to budge on the sentence. He would recommend life in prison without the chance of parole.

Dennis had seen it too many times where a defendant would stand their ground, as if *they* were in control. What they didn't realize is that it was Dennis who was in control. Always. He would offer options to the defendants, but even with that, it was Dennis who came up with the plea agreements, not the defendant. The only control they had was whether they would accept what Dennis offered.

In April, seven months after he shot and killed two people and attempted to shoot a third, Dusty Sampson appeared before County Court Judge Evelyn Johannsen to be sentenced on all ten counts of the indictment charges.

By now, Judge Johannsen was very familiar with Dusty. Between the warrants signed during the initial investigation, to the arrests, arraignments and sentencing of his co-defendants, and Dusty's own court appearances, she was happy to be at the final stages of this heinous, senseless crime. The case had been wearing on everybody; the Judge included.

Mac, Coop, Brandon and Patrick were in the courtroom gallery, along with Officers Eve Swanson and Brian Collins. They had all been involved in the case since the night of the homicides. Also present were some of the WET team officers who had helped during the investigation. For some officers, this would be one of the biggest cases of their career, and it was worth taking the time - whether off duty or on - to observe the sentencing.

Two court security guards brought Dusty into the courtroom. He was wearing the orange and white striped jumpsuit of a prisoner. They had shackled his wrists, with the chain wrapped around his waist.

He scanned the crowd and found his mother sitting in the front row. She looked his way, and for a moment, their eyes locked. It was the first time they had seen each other since his arrest, seven months prior. Because of his continued inappropriate behavior, and as a prisoner in solitary confinement, he was not allowed the privilege of visitors. Not that he had any, although his mother had tried to see him on one occasion, but was turned away.

They escorted Dusty to a wooden table in front of the Judge, and he sat down. His attorney, Tom Weiss, was already waiting in the chair next to him. Dusty looked over his shoulder and tried to smile at his mother. She saw him, but didn't return the smile.

Dusty could see the emptiness in her eyes. For the first time since his arrest, he felt ashamed. He turned back to the front of the room, focusing on the Judge while blinking away the tears in his eyes. He swiped at his nose with the back of his hand.

Dusty and Weiss had a few moments to converse quietly together before Judge Johannsen called the court to order. Dusty wasn't paying much attention to the words his attorney was saying. His mind was mostly on his mother. He hadn't realized until now just how much he'd missed her.

The media was also present en masse in the courtroom. Most of them who'd been around for a while were already aware of Judge Johannsen's policies concerning their presence in her courtroom. During trials, she would not tolerate any distractions, whether it was from doors opening and closing or the constant clicking of laptop keyboards. She did, however, allow cameras in her courtroom during brief proceedings like arraignments and sentencings.

"Counselors, are we ready to proceed?" The Judge looked between DA Wozniak and Attorney Weiss.

"Yes, your honor," they answered together. As they stood up, Weiss flicked Dusty on his arm, to indicate that he should also stand. He did.

"Before we hear the sentencing recommendation from the District Attorney, I've been informed that a couple of people would like to speak. I'd like to ask Maria Schumacher, Michael Schumacher's mother, to the podium. Her son was one of the people who lost their lives that night." The Judge looked only at Dusty while she spoke. "I would ask, Mr. Sampson, that you listen closely to her words and the words of the other victims today."

Maria stood at the podium, cleared her throat and began telling the court about her son, how he was the proud father of two young children whom he loved more than life itself. "Michael was the kind of son that any mother would be proud of. His death has shattered this family and we will never be whole again." She turned to Dusty as she said, "I hope you rot in jail."

One of the most emotional victim impact statements came from Michael's teenage daughter. With her voice quivering, she spoke of the night he was killed, when she and her father had gotten into an argument just before he left for work. She said he never liked leaving things on a bad note. "The last thing he said to me was, 'I'm not mad. I love you, princess. We'll talk more in the morning.' Little did I know, that would be the last time we would ever talk and the nightmare was just beginning."

Judge Johannsen scribbled something in a notebook as she took a few moments to compose herself. From the tears that were flowing in the gallery, she knew that others needed a few moments as well.

The Judge asked David Hamlin's family to come up next. David's mother was too distraught to speak, but his father stood at the podium with her standing next to him. He unfolded a paper he'd pulled from his pants pocket. With a firm voice, he spoke lovingly of their son. He explained that they had adopted David when he was only two days old, after they'd waited nine years for a child.

"Dusty Sampson has destroyed not only my family but also his younger brother's life. He cannot work because he's riddled with anxiety and paranoia. He's angry, lost, and unable to move on with his life.

"The world would never be the same, now that David is dead. All because you needed drug money. You planned it all out, the gun, the driver, and the place to get the cash that you wanted. You had no regard for the lives that you took that night or the people that are left to cope without them."

Next, Judge Johannsen asked Natalie Petrenko to address the Court, for what would be her fourth victim impact statement. Her boyfriend, David Hamlin, had been killed by Dusty Sampson, who then turned the gun on her and attempted to kill her.

"Dusty Sampson, you will never know the pain that you've inflicted on people because of your selfishness. You took the lives of two wonderful people. You've left two children without a father and me without a fiance. None of our lives will ever be the same.

"I spend my nights afraid of going to sleep because my brain plays that night over and over again. The nightmares won't stop. I'm afraid to leave my house, because there might be another evil person waiting around the corner to kill me. You will never, ever understand the damage you've done to so many good people. You are an evil human being and I, too, hope you rot in jail."

With that, the District Attorney was called to approach the bench. He stood at the podium, and the courtroom became quiet again. "Your honor, last September, Dusty Sampson needed cash to pay off his debts and to buy more drugs. Most people would get a job, but not Dusty Sampson. He had tried working at a few jobs, but found that he didn't enjoy working. Well, not many people do, but when we have bills to pay and families to care for, we get a job.

"Dusty preferred stealing to working. So he made arrangements to acquire a gun and made arrangements to get a ride to Rosalee's Restaurant, intending to rob them. He picked Rosalee's because he actually had a job there for a short period of time, so he knew it was a restaurant that had a lot of customers and made a decent amount of money on a Friday night. He knew the layout of the restaurant and he knew the employees, his former co-workers. So that night, he had a buddy drive him to Rosalee's and told that buddy he would pay him after.

"Dusty went inside the restaurant, pointed the gun at the manager, Michael Schumacher, and ordered him to open the safe, which he did. And then Dusty shot him in the head. For no reason at all. He shot and killed Michael in cold blood. Then he turned the gun on David Hamlin, who was lying unarmed on the floor of the restaurant. Dusty Sampson shot him in the head and killed him, too. He tried to kill Natalie Petrenko by putting the gun to her head, but thankfully, the gun jammed. Natalie was able to run away from Dusty and hid in the office. She had no choice but to hide in the office next to the body of Michael Schumacher until the police arrived.

"Over these last several months, I offered several opportunities for Dusty Sampson to accept a plea deal. I didn't like doing that, believe me, but that is my job as District Attorney. He rejected every offer, using the excuse that he was suffering from mental illness, as well as drug and alcohol addictions, and therefore wasn't responsible for his actions that night. Mr. Sampson also tried to claim that while he was incarcerated, he was going through drug and alcohol withdrawal and therefore should be given preferential treatment, and not be punished with solitary confinement. He failed to realize that solitary confinement was used as a punishment for his unacceptable behavior, not his withdrawal issues. When you throw urine at the guards and pick fights with the other inmates, you will be punished. This is true for all inmates, not just the poor, misunderstood Dusty Sampson.

"Nevertheless, if there was any question of his mental state, I did what the law required me to do and had him evaluated. The psychiatrist evaluated him and determined that Dusty Sampson could fully understand the charges that were brought against him, that the drugs and alcohol did not prevent him from understanding right from wrong.

"Your honor, Dusty Sampson has a complete and total disregard for human life. It's as simple as that. Because of that, I am recommending that Dusty Sampson be sentenced on all ten charges of the indictment to life in prison without the possibility of parole. He should never again walk the streets of Gaithersburg as a free man.

"I understand that the federal government has stepped in and indicted Dusty Sampson on their own charges and will seek the death penalty. After today's sentencing, my office will relinquish jurisdiction to the federal government, so that the federal sentence will run at the end of any sentence given in Court today."

Dennis turned to look at Dusty and said, "whatever heart you have beating in your chest, it is not a human one."

Finally, she looked at Dusty and announced that she was ready to announce the sentence. "You are hereby remanded to prison for life, with no chance of parole. As agreed upon with your previous guilty plea and as a term of this sentence you are also giving up your right to appeal this sentence. Dusty Sampson, get the hell out of my courtroom."

The guards wasted no time in escorting Dusty out of the courtroom. He was now an inmate in the custody of the Maryland Department of Public Safety and Correctional Services as a sentenced prisoner for the rest of his life.

Chapter Twenty-Four

Although he was now sentenced to serve the rest of his life in prison on the state charges, Dusty was still awaiting trial on the federal charges, and was therefore considered a federal prisoner. He would not be brought to prison yet, but would stay in the County jail until the federal case was resolved. Dusty went right back to the Montgomery County Correctional Facility.

They placed Dusty in the general population in the hopes that he'd learned his lesson and would behave. That would prove to be a short-lived hope.

Before the ink was dry on his commitment papers, Dusty was back to his old tricks, picking fights with other inmates, being disruptive by constantly yelling for the guards at the top of his lungs and throwing toilet water with urine when the guards attempted to quiet him down. Dusty had even spat on a guard who was bringing him to the outdoor yard for his daily hour of exercise. Once again, he was moved to solitary confinement.

While in solitary, Dusty continued to be unruly. It wasn't long before he wore out his welcome in Montgomery County. As a federal prisoner, he could be housed anywhere in the state, so the feds made arrangements to transport him to the Frederick County jail. Within a couple of months, the Frederick County jail decided they didn't want him either.

The U.S. Marshals Service, which finds housing for federal inmates, contacted the sheriff of Prince George's County to see if they could bring Dusty to his facility. The sheriff agreed, only because the federal government would compensate the county with daily boarding fees.

Eventually, the sheriff of Prince George's County found that Dusty's hostile and combative behavior wasn't worth the money the feds were paying for his room and board. He had his own prisoners' safety, as well as his guards' safety, to consider. The sheriff requested that Dusty be taken somewhere else. It seemed that nobody wanted him.

In the meantime, Dusty's federal attorneys were finding it difficult to travel all over the countryside to meet with their client, especially since he'd been housed at three different facilities within the last eight months. They filed a request with the federal judge to have Dusty transported back to Montgomery County. The judge grudgingly agreed.

·　　·　　·　　·　　·

On a chilly Tuesday afternoon in late January, just over a year since the homicides, the federal marshals brought Dusty back to the Montgomery County jail. He was brought into the facility and, even though he'd been there before, he was processed as a newly arrived inmate. Because of his known hostile attitude, there were plenty of guards on hand to make sure he didn't cause any problems while they fingerprinted and photographed him.

Dusty looked at the guards that were congregated in the booking room on his behalf. One man, standing in a far corner, caught his attention. Dusty stared at the man, sure he knew him from somewhere. The guard stared back, his face turning ghostly white, with a look of surprise on his face.

The guard who was trying to take his fingerprints tugged on Dusty's hand, bringing his focus back to the task. A moment later, Dusty looked over his shoulder to find that the man was no longer standing in the corner. Still, Dusty had the sense that he'd seen that man before.

Dusty was taken directly to solitary confinement. This time, they weren't even going to try putting him in the general population. Dusty laid on his mattress on the floor with his fingers interlocked behind his head. He stared at the ceiling, thinking about the guard he'd seen in the booking room. Maybe he looked familiar from one of the other times Dusty was in this jail, but Dusty didn't think so. He couldn't shake the feeling that he should recognize the man, but no matter how hard he tried to place the face, he just couldn't come up with an answer.

Two days later, that same guard appeared in front of Dusty's cell. Dusty had been sitting on the small bench bolted to the back wall when he looked up to see the guard staring at him from the other side of the metal bars.

"Hello, Dusty," said the guard.

"Who the hell are you?"

"You don't know me?" asked the guard.

"No. Should I?" Dusty was trying to hide his curiosity by feigning disinterest.

The guard looked at Dusty for several moments before taking a deep breath and finally answering him. "I'm your father."

Dusty couldn't believe what he heard. He swung around on the bench and brought his feet to the floor. "What did you say?"

"I said, I'm your father." The man never took his eyes off Dusty.

"You're full of shit." Dusty's voice was just above a whisper.

"I'm serious, Dusty. I'm your father. Earl Sampson. It's been a lot of years since we've seen each other."

Dusty remained quiet. He didn't know what to say to this man who claimed to be his father, this man he hadn't seen in almost twenty years.

"I want you to know, I tried to see you a bunch of times after I left, but your mother wouldn't let me. Did she tell you?"

Dusty didn't answer him.

"Yeah, well, I didn't think she would. She was pretty pissed off when I left," said the prison guard who was claiming to be Dusty's father.

"Why did you leave?" Dusty felt like a four-year-old kid again.

"I remember that day like it was yesterday. Your mother and I had a huge fight. I took off to cool down, like I usually did when we argued, but when I came back a few hours later that night, she wouldn't let me in the house. I told her I wanted to see you, but she wouldn't let me in. She said you were sleeping. I really wanted to push the issue, but I didn't want to wake you, so I thought it would be better if I just left. I figured I would come back the next day when she calmed down.

"I always thought she'd let me back in, but she refused. For a long time, I tried. I really did. By then, I knew that she wouldn't take me back, but for months, I called to see if she'd at least let me talk to you, even if it was just on the phone, especially on your birthday and at Christmas. She said you didn't want to see me. Finally, I gave up. If you didn't want to see me, I would not force you to.

"I never said that. I was four when you left! Damn it, I needed you!" Dusty yelled.

"I know. I needed you too, Dusty. I even drove by the house a couple of times, but one time she caught me. She said if I didn't leave you guys alone, she'd find another place to live and wouldn't tell me where you were. So, I bought another truck - one that she didn't recognize - and I started driving by the house every week or two. Sometimes you were out in the front yard playing with your Matchbox cars in the dirt. At least I got to see you, to make sure you were okay."

Dusty just stood there staring at his father, the steel bars separating them.

"Listen, I have to go. They'll be wondering where I am," Earl said. "I, um, haven't told them I'm your father."

"Why not? Are you ashamed of me?" Dusty sneered.

"Hell, no, Dusty," his father tried to explain. "I'm not ashamed of you, but I've got to be honest. I obviously don't like what you did. Killing people is a horrible thing to do. But that's not the problem. The problem is that we're related. If they find out, I'll get sent to another facility. They frown on having relatives guard the inmates, especially close relatives, like a father and son."

"Yeah, I guess I can understand that," Dusty said.

"I mean it, Dusty. If they find out, I'll get sent somewhere else. If you don't say anything, at least I'll be able to see you once in a while. We have to be careful, though. I'm putting my career on the line."

"Whatever," said Dusty. "I haven't had a father in all this time. I guess I can do without one for a while longer."

Earl fist-bumped the bars of Dusty's cell, and went back to his position with the general population, his steps a bit lighter. For the first time in almost two decades, he had talked to his son.

As time went on, Earl would visit Dusty in solitary confinement while trying not to draw unnecessary attention to the visits. However, once the initial shock of seeing his father again was over, Dusty was not very receptive to Earl's visits. He had harbored too much resentment over too many years to change now. Still, Earl tried to reconnect with his son as often as he could, hoping that Dusty might, eventually, feel differently towards him.

Chapter Twenty-Five

Dusty's federal attorney, Louis Perkins, was trying to work out a plea deal that would save Dusty's life. However, the federal prosecutor, Arlene Metcalf, was adamant that the death penalty remain on the table. After months and months of finagling back and forth, they finally came to an agreement.

Dusty would plead in front of Federal Judge Mortimer Abrahms in August. It was one month shy of the second anniversary of the robbery at Rosalee's Restaurant, where Dusty had already been convicted at the state level of killing two people and attempting to take the life of a third.

The family members of the victims, law enforcement officers from federal, state and local agencies, including Mac and Coop, the media and curious onlookers, packed the courtroom. The Judge allowed the media to remain, but they were to refrain from videotaping the proceedings.

Dusty was brought into the courtroom wearing the traditional jail jumpsuit and sneakers without shoelaces. As usual, they handcuffed him with a chain that wrapped around his waist and prevented him from moving his forearms more than a few inches. If he had an itch on the top of his head, he would have struggled to scratch it.

This time, he did not look in the gallery for his mother.

The Judge allowed Dusty a few moments to speak to Attorney Perkins before the proceedings began. Although Perkins was whispering to his client, Dusty was getting louder and louder.

Mac nudged Coop with his elbow and tossed his head towards Dusty. Coop understood the hint and glanced to the defense table, where Dusty and Louis Perkins were having what appeared to be a heated conversation.

As trained law enforcement officers, Mac and Coop watched the exchange with a heightened sense of awareness. If Dusty got combative, there were plenty of federal marshals and court security officers in the courtroom that would handle the situation. Still, they watched Dusty closely.

"This is bullshit," Dusty said, loud enough for most of the courtroom to hear. "What difference does it make if they sentence me to the death penalty or give me life in prison? With a sentence like that, I'll die in prison, anyway!"

"Listen to me, Dusty," Perkins said. "We've already talked about this. Do you really want to die with a needle in your arm within the next few years? At least this way, you can stay alive and live to a ripe old age."

"Who wants to live to a 'ripe old age' in prison? I told you, I wanted to get out of prison someday. I don't want to be stuck here forever."

"Then you shouldn't have killed two people, Dusty. It's as simple as that. The state charges alone will keep you in prison for the rest of your life. At least now you won't get a lethal injection from the Feds."

Dusty sat at the table, staring at the floor. If he had been a cartoon, smoke would have been coming out of his ears.

Judge Abrahms had watched the exchange between the defendant and his attorney. After a short time, he asked, "Counselor, are we all set to proceed?"

"Yes, your honor." Perkins stood up while Dusty hesitated, then stood a few moments later. Dusty would not look at his attorney or the Judge, but kept his eyes downcast. His face was red from the top of his forehead to below his shirt collar.

Judge Abrahms allowed the families of victims, Michael Schumacher and David Hamlin, to speak, as they had in previous court proceedings. Dusty remained unmoved by the tears and words that were directed towards him. In fact, it looked to Mac as if he was even angrier now than he was when they first brought him into the courtroom.

Federal prosecutor Arlene Metcalf addressed the court by recounting the horrendous crimes committed by the defendant, Dusty Sampson. "Today's sentencing of Dusty Sampson marks the end of a horrific crime that senselessly took the lives of two innocent people. While nothing can ever make up for their loss, we hope that the life sentences imposed on Sampson today represent some measure of justice and will further ensure that he never again is free to victimize anyone else. Our thoughts today are with all four victims, their families, friends and co-workers. All have suffered grievously from the robbery and murders committed by Dusty Sampson."

Suddenly, Dusty yelled out. "Why don't you just shut the hell up! You're a bitch! You're nothing but a bull dyke bitch!"

Perkins grabbed his client's arm and told him, "Knock it off. You need to stop, Dusty!"

"I don't give a shit. This is total bullshit."

Judge Abrahms banged his gavel on the bench. "Counselor, you need to control your client. If you can't, I'll have him removed."

"I'm trying, your honor." Perkins turned back to Dusty and spoke to him, but Dusty continued his rants, clearly not listening to his attorney. Someone from the audience began shouting at Dusty, so Dusty turned to face that individual.

Another heated exchange was now taking place, this time between Dusty and the audience member, who must have known one of the victims. Court security rushed to quiet the person in the gallery.

A few of the federal marshals who had been waiting along the side wall approached Dusty. Perkins instinctively stepped back as a marshal stood in front of Dusty, and two others stood at either side. The marshal in front calmly yet firmly told Dusty he would have to behave himself in Court, or he would be removed. Dusty looked from one to another marshal, and finally closed his mouth, his lips pinched into a thin line. His breaths were coming in brief spurts, like a bull ready to charge the red flag.

The marshals retreated to stand along the side wall again. Perkins took the position next to his client again. "Sorry, your honor. It won't happen again."

Judge Abrahms asked Arlene to take a seat and began speaking. "In order to maintain some decorum in my court, I will now impose the sentence. Mr. Sampson, you have shown absolutely no remorse for your actions the night you took two lives and attempted to take a third. You have shown in more ways than I can count that you have a complete disregard for others and a disregard for human life. You have assaulted and threatened custody division officers in every facility where you've ever been incarcerated. Rarely, in all my years on the bench, have I seen someone like yourself who's shown such uncontrolled and explosive anger.

"You had previously pled guilty to the federal charges of one count of robbery and two counts of using a firearm in furtherance of a crime of violence and murder. To the charge of robbery, you are hereby sentenced to twenty years in prison. On each of the two counts of using a firearm in a crime, you are hereby sentenced to life in prison. These charges are to be served consecutively.

"In the event that the state of Maryland ever releases you, you will be surrendered to federal authorities to serve each of the three sentences handed down today." And with that, Judge Abrahms pounded the gavel on the bench with a resounding bang that echoed throughout the courtroom. The sentencing of Dusty Sampson for the federal charges was now finished.

Dusty Sampson will never, ever be a free man again. He will die in prison.

CHAPTER TWENTY-SIX

Dolores Sampson had been in the federal courtroom for her son's sentencing. To see Dusty being brought into the courtroom in handcuffs and a prison jumpsuit was devastating, and her heart was breaking. Never in her wildest dreams did she ever believe he was capable of murder.

It was a bittersweet moment when she heard the Judge deliver the sentence. Bitter because it meant that he would never get out of prison. Sweet because it meant that he would not die in a few years from lethal injection or the electric chair. No mother wants to see her child die, regardless of the circumstances.

As long as he was still in the Montgomery County jail, Dolores knew she would need to go see him. It was only a matter of a few days before he would be transported from the county jail to a state prison facility to begin serving his life sentence. Once that happened, she did not know when she would have the opportunity to see him again.

The day after the federal sentencing, Dolores went to see Dusty. Although he was still in solitary confinement and visitors were not usually allowed to see prisoners in solitary, the guards allowed Dusty to have a few minutes with his mother. As the guard brought him from his cell to the visitor's room, he let Dusty know that they were doing it for her sake, not his.

As Dusty sat in the cubicle with a plexiglass sheet separating him and his mother, it surprised him to see how much older his mother looked. They both picked up the phone's handsets to talk.

"Hey, Mom. How are you doing?"

"Not good, Dusty, but at least it's almost over. Once we find out where you'll be going, that'll be the end of this whole mess. From here on out, you'll just be serving your sentence. You won't have any more court dates and lawyers."

"Yeah, I guess that's true."

There was a small passage of time when neither one spoke, as if they were struggling to find something to talk about.

"Listen, Mom, I need to ask you something. Why didn't you tell me about Dad?"

This was the conversation she'd been dreading, and the reason she hadn't wanted to visit Dusty in jail for almost two years.

"What about your father?" she asked, her voice barely above a whisper, her face getting pale.

"I saw him. He works here at the prison. Why didn't you tell me all those years ago, when I was still a little kid, that he wanted to see me? You never told me that. Why?"

Dolores picked at a non-existent crumb on the worn counter top of the cubicle and shook her head. "I don't know, Dusty. I guess I was just mad at him. He walked out on us and I wanted to punish him."

"He said he kept asking to see me and you wouldn't let him. He drove by the house and you told him you'd move away and never tell him where we were." Dusty's voice was cracking. "Why would you do that?"

"Like I said, I was mad. I found out he had a girlfriend, so I kicked him out. He was cheating on me." A single tear slid down Dolores' cheek and hung for a moment from her chin before it fell onto her shirt.

"I needed him, mom. I was just a little kid, and I needed him."

"Dusty, I'm sorry. I'm sorry I kicked him out and kept him from seeing you, but I was hurt. I don't want to talk about him anymore."

Dusty sat there, looking at his mother with a blank expression. Neither one seemed to know what to say.

"So, um, listen, Dusty," Dolores finally said. "You'll have to let me know where they take you, okay? Hopefully, it won't be too far away, so I can still come and visit you."

"Yeah, I'll tell you what... I'll have dad call you." Dusty slammed the handset onto the cradle and stood up, the chair sliding backwards with a loud screech.

He stood at the door with his back to his mother, as the guard opened the door of the visitor's room and escorted him back to his cell.

Dolores didn't even breathe for a few moments as she watched her son, her only child, turn his back on her and leave. Slowly, she set the phone down.

Over time, Dolores would make a few attempts to see her son in prison, but he always refused to see her. She begged the guards to bring her son to see her, but they gently told her they couldn't force him.

Finally, one day, the hurt, the pain, and the loneliness became too much. She found a way to escape all of it through the drugs and alcohol that she had always abhorred.

When she had her gallbladder removed a few years earlier, the doctor prescribed morphine. The bottle was full, since she hadn't taken any after her surgery. She also bought a bottle of whiskey. Combined, it was enough to do the job.

Dolores was found two days later when she didn't show up to work. She was lying on the couch, an empty prescription bottle and a half-full whiskey bottle on the table next to her. Across her chest, she clutched a sixth-grade photo of Dusty.

About the Author

The Dusty Road to Homicide is LeeAnne James' fourth novel. Her first novel, *Murder at Gatewood*, was a Central New York Fiction finalist. Her second book, *Bunny Byrd, Amateur Detective* is a fun and cozy mystery. Her third novel, *Justice for Loretta* received both an honorable mention from the 2023 Eric Hoffer Awards in the Mystery/Crime category, as well as being named to the Grand Prize Short List. It was also listed as a finalist in the 2022 American Writing Awards in the Fiction - Mystery/Suspense category and is a five-star recipient from Readers' Favorites.

LeeAnne James lives in Central New York with her husband, son, rescue dog and rescue parakeets. Besides writing, she enjoys her full-time job as the Administrative Clerk for the local police department.

Don't miss the beginning of
The Thin Blue Line Series

LeeAnne James

JUSTICE
for Loretta

THE THIN BLUE LINE SERIES

Note From the Author

Word-of-mouth is crucial for any author to succeed. If you enjoyed *The Dusty Road to Homicide*, please leave a review online—anywhere you are able. Even if it's just a sentence or two. It would make all the difference and would be very much appreciated.

Thanks!
LeeAnne James

We hope you enjoyed reading this title from:

BLACK ROSE
writing™

www.blackrosewriting.com

Subscribe to our mailing list – *The Rosevine* – and receive
FREE books, daily deals, and stay current with news about
upcoming releases and our hottest authors.
Scan the QR code below to sign up.

Already a subscriber? Please accept a sincere thank you for
being a fan of Black Rose Writing authors.

View other Black Rose Writing titles at
www.blackrosewriting.com/books and use promo
code
PRINT to receive a **20% discount** when purchasing.